I0517259

After having his love tossed back in his face, Hudson Sug-gashie has eliminated the word trust from his dictionary. Since his return to his Ojibway community, his suspicions are running high, all because one man is hinting at a second chance — the too-gorgeous and sexy ball-crusher who turned Hudson's world to black fifteen years ago.

Stephen Brandt knows he screwed up big time when he rejected Hudson's love, and he'll do anything to win him back, even if it means being a mere bed buddy to the man whose love he aches to reclaim.

The longer the former best friends engage in their no-strings affair, they want something more — what they lost as teenagers. But Hudson isn't about to open his heart again, leaving a desperate Stephen searching for a way to earn back the trust he broke, or for the second time, they'll lose the greatest love either has ever experienced.

The unauthorized reproduction or distribution of this copy-righted work is illegal. Criminal copyright infringement, including infringement without monetary gain, is investigated by the FBI and is punishable by up to 5 years in federal prison and a fine of $250,000.

This book is a work of fiction. Names, characters, places, and incidents either are products of the author's imagination or are used fictitiously. Any resemblance to actual events or locales or persons, living or dead, is entirely coincidental.

Back Where You Belong
Copyright © 2022 Maggie Blackbird
ISBN: 978-1-4874-3677-3
Cover art by Martine Jardin

All rights reserved. Except for use in any review, the reproduction or utilization of this work in whole or in part in any form by any electronic, mechanical or other means, now known or hereafter invented, is forbidden without the written permission of the publisher.

Published by eXtasy Books Inc

Look for us online at:
www.eXtasybooks.com

Back Where You Belong

By

Maggie Blackbird

DEDICATION

For those who love radio and music as much as I do.

Thanks to my husband and the Mals for their never-ending support.

Another thank you to Emmy, my editor, Bri, my proofer, Martine, my cover artist, and Jay, EIC. I couldn't do this without your help.

CHAPTER ONE—THE SOUND OF YOUR VOICE

If Hudson's grandmother walked into his office at the nursing station, she'd call him a glutton for punishment. Yep. That's exactly what Kokum would say. She'd spoken her mind before her passing last year, and she'd have spoken it again if she'd witnessed him tuned in to Stephen Brandt's radio show blaring from the computer speakers, instead of focusing on the pile of paperwork every nurse practitioner encountered. If he didn't get his act together, he'd be here until midnight, hanging out with the night shift RN.

He glanced at the clock hanging on the wall covered in posters that offered various medical advice. At least Stephen's show ended soon.

If not for the music, the building of four patient beds, two examining offices, a diabetic care room, small medical lab for RNs to take blood, and a reception area, would be deathly quiet at ten to ten.

"As always, I gotta do a cover. Since Jim Dandy is one of my favorite singers, I'm going to let you guess the song. If you think you know who originally wrote and recorded it, be sure to whisper it in my ear." Stephen lightly laughed, a flirty chuckle ghosting the back of Hudson's neck.

He shucked aside his pen. Nothing had changed. The only time Stephen found the courage to flirt was over the airwaves where nobody could stare into his eyes.

Still, Hudson's fingers were about to betray him by

sneaking a message through the radio show's website. Nope, they wouldn't, not after vowing to himself he'd never fall for Stephen again, so Hudson tucked his hands beneath his thighs before the hungry digits betrayed him.

His ears drank in the luscious voice coming from the pilot of the airwaves. Smooth. Fingertips skimming his spine. A massage to the shoulders capable of lulling him to sleep. In the past, it'd been Stephen's steamy breaths brushing Hudson's earlobe with horny declarations sexy enough to feel up every sensitive spot on his body.

He withdrew his hands from beneath his thighs and smacked the desk's top. Oh man, he was doing it again — behaving like a lovesick, seventeen-year-old, insecure idiot. Time to take a well-prescribed pill of chill. There'd be no stinking thinking, not after he'd promised on the plane ride to Moose Lake back in September to give his personality an overhaul instead of behaving like a scorned ex-boyfriend.

Concentrate on the song. You know the riff. That wah wah *is way too familiar.* And groovy enough in a classic rock sense to get Hudson's foot tapping and head bopping. When the growling voice kicked in with the funky lyrics, he snapped his fingers. *Post Toastee* by Tommy Bolin.

He scooted his rolling chair along the floor and stopped in front of the computer. His fingers almost hit the keyboard to type the answer to Stephen's inbox, but Hudson stopped cold.

They weren't teenagers or the best of friends anymore.

Hudson slumped and extended his legs, crossing them at the ankle, blankly staring until the song ended.

"I'll leave you with a favorite of mine," Stephen announced in the same breathy voice that had massaged Hudson's shoulders earlier. "Have a great night and thanks for listening."

If he played *Back Where You Belong* for the fifth time in the past two weeks, he'd end his show with that song.

Sure enough, the regret-filled tenor wailing from the

computer's speakers was the track Hudson had predicted. A man full of sorrow, after he'd turned away the one who truly loved him because he'd been unable to commit at the time, sang about his heartbreak. Following many failed relationships, the man understood he'd walked away from the best love he'd ever known. Now the guy begged for a second chance.

The old Hudson wouldn't believe such a song was meant for him and had nothing to do with the past, when Stephen had volunteered at the reserve's former radio station for Youth Night, ending each broadcast with a special song for Hudson. As for today? He'd bet his ration of firewood—to heat his house through the cold winter—this was Stephen's way of saying he wanted a second chance.

Hudson tapped the pen against his mouth. Maybe he should cease the *looking at you, looking at me* game they'd engaged in whenever Stephen stopped by the nursing station to pick up his mother's medications. With the ice road open and Hudson's truck still stored at a garage six hours south in Red Lake, this was the perfect opportunity for them to reconnect, for him to feel out Stephen and see if he was still a shmuck or not.

They were sharing the same community and couldn't keep up their game of *I see you but I don't*. At least they could be friends, something Hudson had thought long and hard about on the plane ride back to the reserve, knowing when he landed, he'd have to face the man who'd crushed his heart fifteen years earlier.

No. He couldn't ask for a ride into town. With his luck, Stephen would think Hudson was still carrying a torch.

Or maybe he should. The temperature was a good minus thirty Celsius, and he couldn't continue asking his co-workers for rides.

During his confounding deliberation, line two rang, which

3

was strange. The call should've automatically come in on line one. Someone who was purposely dialing the nursing station knew the secondary number.

Before the nighttime RN answered, he snatched up the receiver. "Nursing station. Hudson speaking."

The person on the other end cleared his throat.

Hudson sat up straight. Whenever nervous, Stephen had done the same thing. He'd done so after Hudson had made the biggest mistake of his life by choking out those god-awful three words two weeks after high school graduation.

"Hey. It's Stephen Brandt. I hope I'm not bothering you. I know how busy you are."

Hudson blinked. What was up with the big-ass formal introduction? For ten years they'd been best friends. Thank goodness he'd sat since his knees had weakened to rubber. *Back Where You Belong* was meant for him.

Shit, Hudson needed to speak. "S'okay. I'm doing what I do every night. What about you?" Boy, he really had to get a life. Not that much of a life could be found anywhere in a fly-in reserve. At one time he'd loved this place enough to remain in Moose Lake First Nation forever, until he'd gotten his heart stomped and spit on by the very person on the other end of the receiver—

"I finished programming the next broadcast and I'm on my way out." Hope crackled over the wire. "How've you been? I-I keep meaning to ask, but you're usually with a patient or on the phone whenever I stop by to pick up Mom's meds."

Been? Hudson licked his lips. Try tossing and turning in the sheets every night. Try sneaking peaks at the nursing station's main door once the plane arrived with the weekly prescriptions to catch a glimpse of a sexy-ass heartbreaker.

"Good. How about you?" Shit, their conversation was awkward with a capital A. They were two actors reciting lines on stage.

"I'm doing good, too."

To steady his shaking legs, Hudson settled his hand on his knee. He wouldn't mention the song. "Congratulations . . ." Even his vocal cords shook. "Congratulations on making your dream come true. You always wanted to work in radio." *Not that I've been following your show even when I lived in Winnipeg.*

"I love broadcasting." Stephen's voice melted into a big smile. "If it wasn't for Russell, I never would've tried. He was the best mentor anyone could ask for."

Of course. I know what music means to you. "I see you're also deejaying."

"You got it. The students don't seem to mind having an old guy spinning tunes." Stephen's seductive chuckle was his full lips suckling Hudson's neck. "Either way, they're stuck with me. Nobody else has the proper equipment to host a dance."

Hudson shifted and glanced at his pants. If he dared to get a boner through a mere telephone chat, that was it, he was doomed. "How's your mom?"

That dumb question he'd asked smelled of *I don't know what else to say.* As a nurse practitioner, Hudson saw Mrs. Brandt every other week, and nothing had changed there, because the woman was still colder than the Arctic toward him.

"She's managing." The smile in Stephen's voice remained. "When I'm not home to make dinner, I stop by the restaurant and grab something for us to eat. Tonight, it's Charlie's Chicken."

Hudson sank in the chair. How could he hate Stephen? The darned guy had even been nice while tossing out the *I'm sorry, but . . .* It'd been Hudson who'd hollered, yanked on his clothes, and stormed off after having his love rejected. The worst part was, he'd toppled into the lake while trying to make a dramatic exit from the dock where they'd been lying. To further injure his bruised pride, he'd had to be assisted from the water by the very guy who'd cuffed away his love like one of the many black flies that swarmed the reserve during the summer.

Stephen cleared his throat.

Crap, Hudson had been too busy thinking. So much for not behaving like his pathetic former self.

"So . . . I'm calling . . ." Stephen coughed. "I heard through the moccasin telegraph you need a ride into Red Lake to get your truck."

Hudson tossed his pen in the air. No doubt, Stephen planned on asking him if he could pick up something at the pharmacy while in town.

"I'm going in next weekend for supplies. If you want, you can . . ." Stephen coughed again. "You can c-atch a r-ride. It'll save you airfare. We can split the gas."

Being cooped up inside Stephen's SUV for six hours would be an insane road trip, but Hudson really needed his truck, and nobody else was offering to give him a hand, which left him with no option but to fly in and get it.

This was the test of all tests—seeing if he could stick to friendship and not a dime more. There were only two thousand people on the reserve, and like it or not, he'd be running into Stephen more than at the nursing station if Hudson finally stopped being a hermit and went somewhere else other than work or home.

Remember, you're not a lovesick kid anymore. "Sure."

"Great." The smile reappeared in Stephen's voice. "If I make a weekend trip, I head out on Saturday around seven-thirty to catch the daylight. I stay overnight at the Balmertown Inn and drive back on Sunday."

Whoa. Hold up. Hudson swallowed. Was Stephen hinting to share a hotel room? *Back Where You Belong.* This phone call wasn't a fluke. He was asking for another chance.

Hudson's breathing accelerated. What should he say? *Fuck off? Oh, I can get my own room. Err . . . wanna fuck?* "Uh . . . sure."

6

"Unfortunately, online booking isn't available. You have to phone to book a room. Try typing in Balmertown Inn, Red Lake, Ontario. I already reserved mine."

The breath Hudson let out was so strong, it probably carried through the wire. Okay, Stephen wasn't hinting for a hookup. They could do this—get along and share the same community. Never mind that Hudson's heart pinched at a considerate offer instead of one with a hidden motive of cajoling him into bed. "Gotcha. I'll call there tomorrow."

"Don't forget. The hotels book up fast when the winter road's open. People from the southern reserves go in a lot more often. Usually every weekend. I gotta go."

"Gotcha. I'll call first thing tomorrow morning. Talk to you later." Hudson set down the phone. He could do this. He could take complete control and not fall for a heartbreaker a second time.

Somehow, he'd find the strength to leave the past where it belonged. This was his first true test of the new and improved Hudson two point five.

Stephen fist-pumped his hand as he set down the receiver at the old shack where Russell had first introduced him to radio. He'd done it—made the phone call. Sinking back in the chair, he ran his hands through his hair. For sure he'd believed Hudson would tell him to *fuck off*. Rightly so after he'd screwed up big time. Who wouldn't be angry after coughing up the courage to say *I love you* and hearing crickets?

He'd never put an offer on the table before. And there'd been nothing to be afraid of. Hudson had been friendly during their chat. With the way he'd yelled at Stephen fifteen years ago, he'd anticipated a *kiss my ass, jerk* said in true Hudson style.

Well yeah, Stephen did want to kiss Hudson's ass, but not

while receiving a snarky *take a hike.*

When Hudson had returned to the reserve in September, Stephen had made sure there wasn't a significant other poking around. Through the moccasin telegraph, he'd heard Hudson and the guy he'd been living with in Winnipeg had broken up eight months before he'd moved back after the death of his grandmother.

Stephen reached for his parka. Once he shut down the lights and turned off the equipment at the reserve's former radio station, where they allowed him to broadcast his Internet show, he hustled down the path to his vehicle.

The moon wasn't out, but the stars twinkled above. Clear sky. Not a cloud present meant a below-thirty-Celsius night.

His boots made squashing noises against the shoveled snow. The freezing weather kept threatening to sneak through the heavy material covering him. As for his face, he wasn't experiencing icicles, but sharp bursts of hot stings on any skin not covered.

The cold spell couldn't dampen his spirits, though, only his stomach twisting and turning like spaghetti. Maybe he should've only bought Mom a chicken dinner. This was what he got for not waiting until the morning for daring to do something he'd never done before.

What choice did he have, though? Stopping by the nursing station to pick up Mom's medications to engage Hudson in conversation had proved useless since he'd never approached Stephen to talk. That had left him with no option but to act, and hearing Hudson needed a ride to Red Lake had been the perfect opportunity.

The wind whistled through the spruce trees, the icy air slapping at his face.

Stephen sprinted for his SUV while pressing the button to unlock his running vehicle. He darted inside and leaned in to the driver's side vent. The blasting warmth quickly soothed his frozen skin.

With the stereo already on, music hummed through the speakers since he had the satellite radio tuned to his favorite rock station.

He slid the gearshift into drive and drove off. His conversation with Hudson played out in his mind. His former best friend had asked about Mom. Most important, Hudson had remembered how much Stephen loved music. Maybe Hudson had gotten the hint *Back Where You Belong* was for him? His memory couldn't be bad enough to forget how Stephen had closed his past radio show for Youth Night.

He crossed his fingers. Please let their trip into Red Lake reignite their friendship. They had six hours and the evening to spend together.

Once they reached town, if Hudson questioned why Stephen had no place to be, he'd find another ration of courage and admit the truth—he'd only made the trip to help a friend out. As for the *I hope you give me a second chance* bit, dinner in the hotel dining room could provide them with a great opening to chat about the past.

May the universe pity him so he wouldn't have to resort to begging.

Stephen shook his head. If only time machines existed. He'd dial back fifteen years and change their last night together. Instead of fear dictating his answer, he'd have let his heart speak for him.

CHAPTER TWO: IF I'D BEEN THE ONE

Hudson slung the duffel bag strap over his shoulder. He snatched up his travel mug and tucked the deer-hide mitts Kokum had made for him last Christmas under his arm.

The black SUV, sleek and sexy as Stephen, idled in the driveway. With Stephen being up north in the Seven Mile district and Hudson calling Main home, this was like old times when he'd wait at the window for Mr. Brandt's familiar blue truck to pull up.

Back Where You Belong still played during every radio show. The song couldn't be chalked up to a coincidence, but this past week Stephen had failed to make an appearance at the nursing station. What this all meant, Hudson wasn't sure. Only their drive would provide answers.

He trudged from the house and down the back steps. The chilly air nipped at his face thanks to *Biboon's*—the winter spirit of the Ojibway—cold breaths. It was a good thing he'd packed his balaclava. When would the *manidoo* of the north finally rest and let his brother, *Ziigwan*, arrive? But spring wouldn't happen anytime soon, seeing as it was the middle of January.

Stephen emerged from the SUV, snug as a bug in a black parka and matching boots. "Good morning. A bit cold." He opened the door to the back of the vehicle.

"A bit cold?" Hudson tromped forward. "Compared to up here with this wind chill, the corner of Portage and Main is the Bahamas."

Stephen's eyes sparkled. "C'mon, January's all about the

north wind, and you've been in Win*ter*peg for the last fifteen years. You should be used to this."

"Yeah, you got me there. Fine. But it's colder up here." This was going better than Hudson had expected. They talked like time and their fight hadn't come between them.

Setting his hands on his hips, Stephen flashed his dimples, the boyish indents that Hudson had loved to touch in the past. "Don't try and tell me you didn't expect a long, freezing winter. I'm betting you checked the beehives and the beavers' feed-beds in the fall."

Hudson snickered. "Yep, sure did. But a man has a right to complain now and then, doesn't he?" He set his duffel bag beside the two blue suitcases on the back seat, one probably filled with emergency provisions, because from what he recalled in the past, Stephen wasn't the kind of guy to pack the kitchen sink.

Stephen removed his parka. He placed the big coat on top of the luggage. "I should've remembered you enjoy a good . . . bitch session." He rubbed his biceps." I don't know what's worse. The dry cold or the moist cold."

A whiff of cologne tickled Hudson's nose. Was the scent of spice meant for him? He stomped down the excitement attempting to form. He was here for a truce, not romance. "The moist. It finds its way into your bones." He also removed his parka.

"True." Stephen darted into the vehicle and slammed the door shut.

Teeth rattling, Hudson scurried around the SUV. He wasn't dense. Nobody spritzed on something sexy for a six-hour drive. The fragrance was for him.

He jumped into the vehicle and stole a glance from the corner of his eye. Stephen had donned his sunglasses. Hudson should, too. The reflection from the snow was brighter than diamonds.

Although the cell phone rested in one of the cupholders, music came from the satellite radio built into the stereo system. Naturally, Stephen didn't stream music. A true connoisseur, Hudson knew his ex-boyfriend believed in owning the music and supporting the artist.

Sitting in the vehicle together was like being back in school, when Hudson had ignored his studies and chose to drool in Stephen's direction—a lethal combination of Ojibway and Swedish.

Stephen glanced at the rearview mirror and backed the SUV out of the driveway. He was rather yummy in a blue button-down shirt and jeans that complemented the straight collar-length black hair he'd inherited from his mother. Mrs. Brandt had also gifted him with her black brows, dark lashes, and bronzed skin he kept clean-shaven. As for his red lips, wide shoulders, long legs, and high cheekbones, those came from the late Mr. Brandt. But nothing beat Stephen's piercing blue eyes shining brighter than the sunlight reflecting off the lake in the summer

Hudson quickly glanced toward the side passenger mirror at his round face, full cheeks, small black eyes, and wide, short nose.

Bland. More than bland. He folded his arms. Well, he did have one thing going for him. He'd worked off twenty of the thirty-five pounds he'd put on over the years. Besides pumping iron in the spare bedroom at home, walking everywhere had helped speed up the weight loss process.

After he retrieved his truck, she'd remain parked unless the weather didn't cooperate. Wondering what Stephen had thought of Hudson's extra gut when he'd moved back in September had motivated him to get his potato off the couch.

"Y'know, you used to do that when we were . . ." Stephen cleared his throat.

Hudson refocused his attention to what lay inside the

vehicle. Enough assessing the dullest face on earth. "Do what?"

"Oh . . . uh . . . nothing." Stephen steered them onto Hawk Road.

Knots appeared in Hudson's shoulders. Was he responsible for Stephen's nervousness? "No. Go ahead. I won't mind."

"You'd look at yourself in the mirror and frown." With a trembling hand, Stephen reached for his coffee.

There couldn't be awkwardness between them. They'd been two dumb teenagers when their fight had gone down.

Hudson should kick himself for being insensitive to Stephen's discomfort over his sexual orientation at the time. A true friend would have understood. Not pushed to get his way, coaxing Stephen into more than he'd been comfortable with, and damned if he hadn't pushed back.

Perhaps saying *I love you,* planning their lives together, and demanding they come clean to the Brandts had been too much for Stephen to brave in one night. Hudson had figured if Kokum had accepted his sexual orientation and had even told him about the two-spirit people, everyone would embrace their relationship — even Stephen's super-strict father.

Hudson continued to stare at the banks of snow lining the road and covering the tall spruce trees. White was everywhere, except for the blue sky.

"Hey, I didn't mean to offend."

Hudson slightly jumped. He really had to stay in the present and stop taking trips to yesterday. "You didn't offend. Sorry. Was checking out the area. I haven't been this far south since I got here."

The Sawbuck district of the reserve wasn't a stretch for vehicles, but a good hike if walking.

"Are you sure?" Stephen glanced at Hudson and back to the road.

"Yeah."

Stephen smiled. "You're lucky. Everything is where you live. At times I used to wish we lived in Main."

"The school's in your neck of the woods. A quick walk down the road . . . unless it's colder than a penguin's ass." Hudson settled in the seat. Yep, old times. Maybe there was a chance they'd . . . He squeezed his eyes shut. No, he couldn't go there. Friends and not a dime more. They'd tried once before and had failed. And Stephen could not be trusted.

"You started your radio show after you finished university, hey." There was a great topic. Music was the perfect conversation.

"Actually, I volunteered for the university's radio station first. The grunt work—engineering and editing." Stephen shrugged. "Not that I minded. I enjoy everything about radio. It doesn't matter if I'm on the air or not."

Hudson nodded. Everyone who'd volunteered at the reserve's former radio station had loved listening to Russell. Too bad R-E-D-D had gone under five years ago after Russell's premature death.

"I'm sorry you couldn't take the course at the college." Hudson had spent a long time consoling Stephen after his father had shot down his dream of becoming a deejay.

"Y'know, there's nothing to be sorry about." Stephen used his index finger to rub the steering wheel. "It worked out how it was supposed to work out. Mom and Dad said the school needed teachers, and they were right. I don't regret getting my B.Ed. I enjoy my job."

"You do?" Hudson knitted his brows.

"I still get to broadcast." Stephen again glanced at Hudson and back to the road. "Why not here? I can move my Internet channel wherever I go. I even get to freeform. I'd never be able to pick my own music if I worked at a station in the city. And I deejay whenever there are dances. I had a blast at the New Year's Eve social."

14

Thanks to the man seated beside Hudson, he'd skipped the event. Plus, he hadn't experienced much holiday spirit after losing Kokum, a woman he'd thought of as his mother from the age of seven. She'd taken him in after his dad had died in a barroom brawl in Saskatoon, and his mother had sunk further into alcoholism. When he'd needed a friend most, funny how he and Stephen had become best pals.

"Yeah, the staff at the nursing station couldn't stop talking about it."

"You should have —" Stephen cleared his throat. "Did you go to the 'Peg?"

"No." Hudson sipped the coffee. "I hung out here. Visited my uncle and his wife. Saw a few cousins." He'd passed on Winnipeg because Kokum had always flown in for Christmas. Celebrating in the city without her would have produced too much heartache. "What about you?"

"Was busy. Between the school party, dances, and a trip into Thunder Bay to shop, I'm getting more rest now than I did over the holidays." Stephen chuckled.

"Yeah, your radio program and teaching has you juggling two jobs." Hudson glanced out the window at the roundhouse's roof covered in a thick layer of snow.

The special place with its nine sides represented the clans of the community, and the circular structure embodied the powerful circle, the biggest belief of the *Anishinaabeg* that everything was linked together, right down to the life-and-death cycle. The building was constructed from cedar, a tree sacred to the Ojibway for its protection against malevolent spirits and healing properties, the same for the four poles inside to brace the peaked roof.

Out here alone, only with *Biboon*, the roundhouse didn't appear lonely but accepting of the seasonal cycle, right down to its earthen floor, left bare, so the occupants inside could touch the Great Mother. Keeping with tradition, the two main doors faced east and west.

They came upon the road leading to the powwow grounds that were no doubt blanketed in the white stuff.

Stephen cleared his throat.

Heat stung Hudson's face. How many times had he told himself to stay in the present? Old memories fought to surface anyway—such as when he'd donned the regalia Kokum had made for him and danced while Stephen had sat in the stands and watched.

Attending the powwows in Winnipeg and the surrounding reserves over the years hadn't been the same without Stephen's eyes on Hudson. Maybe because from the age of seven he'd danced for the one he . . .

"I take it you'll be dancing?"

"Yeah." Hudson turned his head because the vehicle had stopped.

Stephen also stared at the snow-covered road leading to the powwow grounds.

"You went to the one this summer?" Hudson asked.

While folding his upper lip over the other, Stephen narrowed his slanted black brows. "Of course."

Take off your freakin' sunglasses. Was Stephen also recalling what they'd shared? Had the annual powwow not been the same because Hudson hadn't been present?

The vehicle rolled away. They merged onto Muskrat Drive and went west.

Hudson rubbed his brow. Only a fool kept searching for dumb signs. Stephen had probably been thinking about something else when he had stopped the SUV.

"Going to university instead of college was a smart move. I met two guys who had their own business. I learned lots from them." Stephen set the coffee mug in one of the cup holders. "When I earned my degree, I worked my ass off to buy my own equipment."

Hudson drummed his fingers on his thighs. Naturally, the Brandts had wanted Stephen to acquire a degree instead of a diploma or a trade license offered by the colleges in Canada. "Heard you had a pretty good business going on the side."

"I was booked almost every weekend. Socials. Weddings. You name it." Stephen's chipper voice matched his big smile.

Hudson clenched his jaw and glared at the landing. Once they hit the ice, it'd be six hours of Stephen babbling about his perfect life. Darn rights he had a life made from cotton candy while Hudson's was spinach. The man had come out at twenty-five and had dated a couple of guys. Talk about a one-eighty, while Hudson had been forced to coax Stephen into holding hands, kissing, touching, and finally getting busy.

"Pick a channel if you want." Stephen handed over a paper. "Just tell the radio what you want to hear."

Hudson grasped the playlist paper. Once he located the number to the seventies glam channel, he asked the Satellite radio to play the music.

The truck moved down the landing and onto the ice. A straight plowed road led to the other shoreline peppered with tall spruce trees.

A *got it* moment went off in Hudson's head. If Stephen had accepted his life as a teacher instead of a deejay, why couldn't Hudson damned well do the same? Hiding out at home and mooning about the past had haunted him like the winter wind as soon as his plane had touched down back in September.

He straightened in the seat. Then there was the promise to himself about starting over. Two thousand people lived on the reserve. At the nursing station last week, two former buddies from high school had asked him to go snowshoeing. It was time to start accepting the invitations.

"I'm gonna stop by the fire hall. See about volunteering." No more hermit Hudson. If Kokum was alive, she'd tell him to quit mourning and start living.

Stephen nodded. "Good idea. They always need help."

"I have to borrow a pair of snowshoes until I can get Stanley to make me a pair. Mark Kakegamic and Richard Meekis invited me out. I saw them at the nursing station. They were picking up their moms' prescriptions. They even asked me to join them at the gym since they know I've been lifting weights at home." The great outdoors and some additional exercise was the right spoonful of medicine.

Stephen's lips moved into a small smile. His high cheekbones brightened to pink. "It shows." He cleared his throat. "You look great."

Hudson stiffened. Had Stephen thought of him as a fat bastard when he'd first returned? Because once he'd peeled off the twenty pounds, the guy had come sniffing around the nursing station.

They started up the other landing.

"I mean you *always* looked great. Okay?" Tension crawled into Stephen's words.

Hudson fastened his gaze on Stephen. "I didn't say anything."

"I know you didn't. But in the past . . . Never mind." Stephen pressed a button on the steering wheel and the volume to the stereo grew louder.

"What about the past?" Hudson manually lowered the volume.

"We have a six-hour drive," Stephen murmured. "Let's not go there."

"Go where?" Fine, Hudson could admit he was being a badger's ass.

Stephen let out a deep breath. "You look great. You've always looked great to me. But do you believe me? I'm betting no. You never did before, so why would you now? Can we move on?"

Where did Mr. Perfect get off talking to Hudson in a

patronizing tone? He shifted in the seat and extended his finger. "Not everyone has the DNA of a male model. Some of us get the *average* gene." *And I had the rotten luck of getting the plain gene.*

"Aw, not this again." Stephen frowned.

"What do you mean—not this again?" Hot knives pricked Hudson's gut.

"I don't want to talk about this. I don't." Stephen snatched his mug from the holder. "We got a lot of ice to cover. I offered to help because we used to be friends. I thought it'd be nice to get together again, but I see—"

"Friends. Yeah. Sure." Hudson couldn't help his snort.

As if Stephen wanted to reawaken the past. As teenagers, when he wasn't being a paranoid scared idiot, they'd spent their evenings and afternoons in one another's arms. Their time together never had to end in sex for Hudson either. He'd loved their quiet talks, both naked and bare flesh touching.

The hot knives faded. An ache surfaced in his chest. He glanced out the passenger window for the bazillionth time.

The SUV slowed and stopped.

CHAPTER THREE: I'M A FOOL FOR YOU

Spruce trees climbing to the sky surrounded them. The only sound was the radio playing softly at the volume Hudson had lowered the stereo to seconds ago. He'd shot off his mouth, and by the suffocating tension inside the vehicle, Stephen was ready to respond.

The wind was picking up, scattering snow across the ice road. Not even a bird appeared. The creatures of the forest must be still hunkered down, not ready to show their faces until the sun was full in the sky.

"Yes. Friends." The gearshift sliding into park made a clicking noise. "We were friends first. Right?"

Hudson squeezed his eyes shut. Not the delicate voice that kissed him in his most sensitive spots.

"Hudson?"

He shifted his attention from the white scenery.

Stephen removed his sunglasses. Pain gathered in his eyes. "I wasn't trying to insult you. I simply agreed you look great. But you've always looked great to me — no matter what. And . . ." He licked his lips. "It always bothered me when you'd put yourself down or compared yourself to me. It confused me, because I like you just the way you are."

Bristles of annoyance prickled Hudson's skin. If he was a big bag of barbecue chips, why toss his love back at him fifteen years ago? He squirmed. Fine, he could accept that being gay had terrified Stephen as a teenager, so coming clean about the true nature of their friendship had left Mr. Tall, Dark, and Handsome shaking in his running shoes. But did *I love you* call for a kick to the balls? No. They could have kept hiding in Stephen's dark closet.

Hudson snorted. What the hell was wrong with him? A couple of minutes ago he'd reminded himself about his vow. It was time to take out the bleach and clean his pissy attitude until it sparkled — starting now.

Being a closed-off bastard had cost him four great guys in Winnipeg. Of course they'd dumped Hudson's commitment-phobic ass because he'd refused to utter those three evil words after having them tossed in his face by Stephen. Spending fifteen years in misery had gotten Hudson nowhere, and he didn't plan on living this way for another fifteen.

"I guess that's for me?" Stephen's voice was melancholier than the beating of the hand drum at Kokum's traditional funeral.

"No. I snorted because of me." Hudson sat straighter. "I'm fine. Let's get going. I need my truck. And thanks for offering to help."

Stephen's lake-blue eyes brightened — if they could get any brighter. Talk about wet water sparkling under the morning sun. "Okay." He shifted the gear into drive.

Hudson scooped his coffee from the holder. When Mr. Brandt had passed away, Stephen had moved home to work at the school and care for his mother. There was no significant other, so he must hook up while in Winnipeg or Thunder Bay.

No, Hudson wouldn't think about Stephen strutting his stuff in the gay bars. Positive thinking was only allowed, otherwise the green-eyed monster would appear.

Chin up. Hudson tilted his chin upward. *Shoulders back.* He straightened his shoulders. They could speak about something lighter, like the group Stephen had started for the two-spirit youth in the community.

"I bet the kids are glad you started a group for them." Hudson finally sampled his coffee.

"They are. I thought it'd be a good idea because . . ." Stephen slid on his sunglasses. "A lot are confused. They're learning to be proud of who they are."

"How many are in the group?"

"Four. Two girls. One boy. And another who identifies as non-binary. The parents and community have been very supportive. Well, almost everyone. One of the girls is having some difficulty with her father, but she should be okay."

Hudson snuck a peek. If that wasn't a slap of déjà vu striking his face, he didn't know what was. The girl's father seemed to have taken a cue from the late Mr. Brandt. Then again, Stephen had said the girl would be okay.

Hudson tightened his grip on the coffee mug. Too bad there hadn't been a youth group led by a two-spirit individual when they'd been kids. If so, life would have turned out different for them. Wrong. His dumb declaration of love had sunk them.

He drew in a calming breath. "Winnipeg has a great two-spirit center. When I first moved, I checked it out. Lots of nice people there."

"I should stop in the next time I visit the 'Peg." Stephen cleared his throat. "You're more than welcome to participate in the group here. We meet every Monday and Friday at four-thirty in my classroom. The elementary part of the school. I know it's kind of a stretch since you're done work then, but it'd be nice to have you on board. You were the one who told me about the two-spirit."

Hudson nodded. "I assumed you believed now. You did start a group for the kids."

Red crept onto Stephen's high cheekbones.

The darned guy should be embarrassed. In a smug voice, he'd quoted his dad by saying the two-spirit was bullshit. Those words had instigated an argument.

"I was wrong to tell you there was no such thing as two

spirits." Again, Stephen cleared his throat. "We've been fundraising so the kids can attend the Indigenous Two-Spirit gathering. It's been a slow process. I went last year and brought back lots of information for them, but it'd be nice if they could also go."

Hudson faced Stephen. "You've changed."

"Changed?" Stephen shook his head. "No. I'd say I bypassed my fear. My biggest regret is not accepting who I am sooner."

Hudson glanced at his hands. "Is that all you regret?"

"No." Stephen let out a deep breath. "There's something else I regret."

Hudson rubbed his chest. Stephen probably meant their sexual relationship. He must, because he'd only talked about their friendship up until now.

Touching this man's hair at fifteen had been Hudson's biggest mistake. No. The mistake had occurred at age seven, when he'd come to Stephen's aid. The school bullies had called him *white boy* and shoved him around. Instant friends afterward. A friendship paid for in pain.

The kids in the two-spirit group needed Hudson's help, though. If he joined, more people might come on board. Plus, he had to honor his promise of getting more involved instead of hiding out at home, absorbed in self-pity. "I'll attend the meetings. I might be a good ten or fifteen minutes late."

Stephen lifted his hand from the gearshift. "Not a problem. You can join in when you get there."

"Sounds good."

"There are only five of us. I have a hunch the kids will enjoy having you there."

"I hope so." Hudson stared at more snow swirling about on the road.

"They will. And thank you." Stephen flashed a big smile. He lowered his chin and quietly added, "I'm also glad you'll be there."

Was Stephen implying . . . Where was the bleach Hudson had thought about earlier? Because it was time to scrub his brain again, or he'd be thinking *those* kinds of thoughts, but his ballooning heart wouldn't listen. "I'm glad it does. All you had to do was ask before. Why'd it be any different today?" His knee quaked.

"Yes, I guess it's not any different, is it?" Stephen licked his lips. "I-I haven't forgotten how generous you are. You're a good friend. I guess I should take lessons from you."

Lessons? "Why would you say that?"

"Because I think you're a better . . . a b-better friend than me. A better person."

Hudson straightened. "Why're you saying this stuff? What brought this on?"

"Maybe I could have been a better friend." Stephen tilted the stainless-steel mug. The coffee must've tasted good, because he let out the smallest *ahh*. "Instead of thinking about myself all the time, I should have . . ." He shrugged. "I guess it's in the past." He pressed the rim against his mouth.

Hudson's heart kept ballooning. What was going on? *Ask, dammit.* Failing to give Stephen a chance to explain in the past was why they sat here as strangers today. "What're you trying to say?"

Stephen's Adam's apple bobbed. He pushed up his sunglasses.

Damn, he had a gorgeous, lean, long neck the right shade of tanned brown. A sexy throat Hudson had kissed many times. Stephen's skin set off against the never-ending white of the ice road and snow, and his irises sparkling like the lake hidden beneath them, was a vision to feast upon.

"I guess what I'm trying to say is . . ." The SUV slowed. Stephen's searching gaze pierced Hudson like a finger lightly poking his chest. "I'm sorry."

"Sorry for what?" Hands trembling, Hudson reached for his own mug. He needed to keep busy or his constant shaking threatened to rattle him apart.

"Sorry for not being a better friend. Sorry for . . . pretty much everything." Stephen once again stared straight ahead. The SUV began to climb a hill with more spruce trees bookending them.

Be a man and accept his apology. Friendship was what Hudson had been after. His problem was the silly signals he kept misreading. "Apology accepted. You didn't have to say you're sorry. It's not your fault. We both wanted different things. Life turned out how it was supposed to turn out."

They were on opposing pages. Heck, different books. There went a chance at picking up where they'd last left off, which was an insane thought, because Stephen couldn't be trusted.

Hudson swigged more coffee. Aw, fuck. He couldn't keep lying to himself or trying to talk himself into something false. Bottom line. He didn't want other guys. He wanted Stephen. He was the only man Hudson had ever wanted and the only man he'd ever want.

Still, if they were to only be friends, there were other ways he could take care of his *needs* that jerking off in the shower couldn't provide enough relief for. His right hand was slowly becoming his new lover. He deserved more than a hand, four fingers, and a thumb. Winnipeg was the answer. Stephen probably knew of bars where a guy could find a buddy for the night since he had come back to the reserve two years earlier than Hudson had. "You, uh, make trips into Winnipeg, right?"

"Yes." A trace of disappointment laced Stephen's voice, which was strange.

"Where do you meet people?" Hudson sipped the coffee and grunted. His Maxwell House had morphed into battery acid.

"Meet people?"

"Yeah. You know. Men. The kind of men who . . . well, want a friend for the night."

"Oh." Stephen sucked in his cheeks. "I see." He slammed the mug into the cup holder. "You want to meet other men in Winnipeg?"

"Yeah." Hudson scrambled to think fast. "It's been, well, me and my ex-boyfriend broke up eight months before I moved here. I'm not ready for a . . ." Yes, relationship was the right word so Hudson didn't sound like a using asshole. "Well, not ready to date again, but you know how it goes . . ." he lied. "A guy has to . . . err . . . see to certain things."

"Certain things? Seriously? Why are you asking me?" Stephen's tone sharpened. "You lived there for the past fifteen years. You should know the spots."

"I don't. I wasn't into picking up guys."

"Then why . . ." Stephen huffed out a breath. "There's a couple of bars and a restaurant. I'll get you the addresses when we're back at the rez."

"Thanks."

Stephen's plush lips flattened and his jaw tightened. He reached over and cranked up the stereo volume.

Hudson set his elbow on the armrest. Great. He'd ticked off Stephen. What else could go wrong during their trip?

CHAPTER FOUR—SAME OLD FEELING

When they reached Lake Manitou, a reserve the ice road cut through, Stephen guided the SUV beside one of the four pumps at the gas bar, a building constructed in the shape of a wigwam, hence its name—Wigwam Gas Bar.

His apology had gone over like an opening band at a rock concert getting booed off the stage. Instead of starting a chat about trying again, Hudson wanted to meet other guys. Maybe Stephen deserved Hudson's indifference after rejecting him fifteen years ago. Time ticked on, and Hudson had ticked along with it, which was what any normal, sane person did.

Stephen almost sighed. At seventeen, he'd blown the chance of a lifetime.

He got out of the vehicle and flung the door shut.

Joe Ataway meandered over, resembling a polar bear in his white snowsuit and balaclava. "Morning. Heading into town, are ya?"

"Yes." Stephen yanked on his toque. "Can you fill it?"

"No problemo." Joe ambled around the SUV.

Stephen reached into the back of the vehicle and snatched his parka, teeth rattling. Even a second of exposure iced his veins, so he quickly pushed his arms into the sleeves of the coat.

Hudson got out. He opened the other door while waving his mug. "Cold. I'm going to get a refill at the restaurant. Did you want one?"

"Sure." Stephen slipped on his gloves. "Thanks." He closed the door and darted toward the store, unable to stop thinking about Hudson wanting to fly into Winnipeg to chase other guys.

Stephen shoved on the store's glass door. Maybe he should offer his body if Hudson was so horny he needed to use someone for a night? At least it'd keep him out of another man's bed.

He stopped in front of the chocolate bar rack. Where did such a crazy idea come from? He'd already vacated his comfort zone enough times. However, thanks to Hudson, Stephen had no choice but to seek more courage. He swerved around a rack of potato chips to reach the counter.

If Hudson balked at the suggestion, Stephen would die of embarrassment and heartbreak. There had to be another solution. He had to make the offer without sounding desperate. Yes, he was desperate, but Hudson didn't have to know.

What if the proposition came from a logical point of view? Such as spending an evening together would save Hudson the cost of airfare and a hotel room? They were gay and lived in the same community. They had needs. How could Hudson say no to common sense?

A woman in her forties stood in front of the pop coolers. The gas bar only carried snack items since the general store in the main part of the reserve supplied groceries. He could purchase coffee here, but Hudson was taking care of refilling their mugs next door at the diner.

Stephen reached into his wallet and withdrew the cards he'd need to pay for his tax-free gas. His stomach muscles clenched. Not again. After he'd called Hudson, Stephen's gut had twisted all week. This morning he'd managed a granola bar. Before he'd bolted out the door, Mom had peered at him in the same suspicious way Dad had in the past when he'd head out for the night with Hudson.

As a teenager, that gauging stare coming from his parents had frozen Stephen's spine into an icicle, which had cost him

Hudson, because he'd been terrified of Dad ascertaining the truth. But mom's assessing gaze wasn't enough to deter him anymore.

Perhaps blow-drying his hair, shaving, spritzing on cologne, and ironing his blue shirt had tipped Mom off to the real purpose of his trip? He should have donned a sweater instead. Thanks to his vanity move of wearing something light instead of bulky to make sure he got more than a once-over from Hudson, Stephen couldn't stay warm.

Joe ambled inside the gas bar. A blast of cold air followed him. He stomped his big boots on the mat. "Brr. Been doing this since six o'clock, yup. You think I'd be used to it." He shucked his deer hide gloves and put them on the counter.

"Sorry to make you go out there."

"No problemo. It's my job." Joe grinned. He grabbed the bank card and status card to ring up the gas order.

Over dinner Stephen would make the offer to Hudson. Friends with benefits. The knife in Stephen's stomach sharpened. He wanted them to be lovers. Not bed buddies. But to have Hudson, Stephen had no choice but to play the game, or he'd watch Hudson fly out to Winnipeg to hump other guys, since he'd more than said he wasn't seeking romance.

There was no way Stephen was allowing someone else to move in on the man he wanted to call his own.

Hudson sank into the vehicle's seat. He tilted the mug to his lips, and the fresh-perked brew rolled down his throat. Just what the doctor prescribed—a nice cup of joe to relax him while the radio played Slade's *Coz I Love You*.

Funny, while everyone else in high school had dug rap, nu-metal, alternative, and industrial, he and Stephen had preferred southern and glam rock, from Molly Hatchet and Black Oak Arkansas to the Sweet and T. Rex. Their teacher, Mr.

Petersson, had introduced them to the former. As for the latter . . .

"*All That Glitters,*" Hudson murmured. He still watched the movie to this day.

"What?" Stephen lowered the volume of the stereo.

"Nothing. Talking to myself." Just like the film, Hudson had wanted them to fall in love and turn their backs on everyone. The movie took place in the early seventies, a taboo time for gay relationships, and by the end of the flick, the two heroes had given up fame and fortune to be together.

"Oh." A hint of disappointment lined Stephen's voice. "I thought you mentioned *All That Glitters.*"

Hudson jumped in his seat. "You remember?" Dumb question. They'd almost worn out the DVD. Fifteen years old. His fourth trip off the reserve, when Stephen had talked his parents into letting Hudson join them in Winnipeg. At the mall, they'd happened upon the movie in the St. Vital neighborhood.

"Uh, yeah." Stephen chuckled. "Why wouldn't I . . . uh . . . it's when . . . ahh . . ."

Hudson sucked in his breath. Thanks to *All That Glitters,* they'd not only discovered glam, they'd discovered each other, since Stephen had finally acknowledged the chemistry simmering between them.

The memory was as fresh and alive as it had been seventeen years ago. While Stephen had trembled, Hudson had brushed his palm along the thick, black strands of his best friend's hair—the very hair Hudson had burned to touch starting at the age of eleven. He'd rubbed the soft strands between his fingers. Close. Their breaths and gazes had even touched. When Hudson had drawn back, shaking, Stephen had glanced down at his lap, still trembling.

Hudson pointed at the stereo. "It's my favorite song."

Although the music had a skip-down-the-road vibe, the

lyrics expressed what he felt for Stephen. No matter what kind of wounds the antagonist inflicted on the protagonist in the song, nothing could discourage the guy's love.

"Slade?" Stephen also pointed at the stereo.

Hudson nodded. The crisp blue sky remained above them. Not one cloud present. The sun was glaring down on the snow, so he'd slipped on his sunglasses earlier.

"They were your group."

"You preferred Roxy Music." A trickle of warmth traveled up Hudson's spine.

"I was all about .38 Special and Black Oak Arkansas." Stephen lightly smiled. "You were into Skynyrd and the Atlanta Rhythm Section."

Back Where You Belong. Hudson's breathing quickened. The song was meant for him. He briefly squeezed his eyes shut. Winnipeg. Hooking up. He'd stay on topic and not go *there*. "Weird how we could dig glam and southern rock, hey?"

"I don't think it's weird. True music lovers have a diverse taste. We're not limited to a specific genre." Stephen glanced at Hudson and back to the endless sea of white. "Kind of like . . . uh, how opposites attract. Who's to say two different people can't . . . get along?"

Correct. Love worked the same way. Hudson rubbed his coffee mug. People dated various personality types, shapes, and races until they found their special someone. "Guess that's why you never married."

"What?" The knuckles of Stephen's hand on the steering wheel whitened. His mouth fell open.

A roar filled Hudson's ears. Holy hell, he'd spoken aloud. He'd been dumb enough to . . . *Get me out of here!* He slammed the mug into the cup holder. His gaze darted around the dashboard. He couldn't bail from a moving vehicle. They still had two hours to go. Walking the rest of the way, to get his truck, he'd freeze to death.

Think, dammit!

"I-I was referring to what you said—when you compared dating to music genres." Hudson's teeth rattled. "We listened-listened to nu-metal and industrial first. Then we switched genres when Mr. Petersson introduced us to southern rock. We switched 'cause neither of us . . . we weren't really into that stuff but we didn't have anything else to listen to until we discovered—"

Hudson swallowed. "Well, until the right genre came along."

"You—You think I never found my right . . ." Stephen cleared his throat. "Genre?"

A zap of heat scorched Hudson's earlobes. "I shouldn't have said that. I didn't mean to. I should be pointing the finger at myself."

Okay, Hudson had managed to stumble through the conversation without resembling a guy stepping in dog shit while trying to impress a hottie. Now he'd go for broke and not only point the finger at himself, he'd poke his chest. Anything to stay away from what he'd said about Stephen.

"I burned through four relationships." Hudson let out a breath. "It wasn't their fault. It was mine. All mine. Live and learn."

"I'm sure you had your reasons." Stephen stared straight ahead. "It takes two, so it can't be all your fault."

"It was." Hudson fiddled with the handle on the mug. "Leonard . . ."

When he'd first arrived in Winnipeg, he'd met the handsome, older volunteer at the Two-Spirit Center. Leonard had provided Hudson with all kinds of information from safe sex to gay bars. Saying yes to a date was something he still regretted because he shouldn't have jumped into a relationship at the time to purge his heart of Stephen. Leonard had been a great guy who'd deserved someone's undivided attention and love. No wonder they'd crashed and burned after a year.

"Leonard?" Stephen sounded like a frog was lodged in his throat.

"Yep . . . Leonard." Hudson rubbed his cheek. "He wanted more, and I wasn't ready. Hell, the same goes for the three other guys I shacked up with."

"Maybe you were ready." Stephen's chest rose and sank. "Maybe—Maybe they were the wrong . . . genre."

"You think so? I guess I should reword and say I tried other genres but I prefer glam."

"You—You do?" Stephen glanced at him.

"Yeah. I . . ." Whoa, hold up. There was no way in hell Hudson would say he *loved* glam. That word was officially off limits. "I prefer glam over any other kind of music."

"What about southern? Southern and glam." Stephen turned back to the road. "They might be opposites, but we made both genres work together. I—I mean we liked both. Still do."

"Yeah, we did, and do, don't we?" They were stepping a tad too close to the fire. Hudson should change the subject, but did he really want to? Maybe if he kept their chattering casual, they'd finally speak about what happened between them fifteen years ago.

He drummed his fingers on his thighs. "You're glam."

Stephen tapped his chest. "Glam? Those guys wore makeup and glitter. They dressed outrageously." He chuckled.

"It's more than makeup and glitter. It's about image, looks, and attitude. A guy couldn't be a plain glam rocker. And he sure couldn't be butt ugly. Southern is—"

"Honest? Relaxing? From the heart?" Stephen rubbed his knee.

Hudson had been about to say Southern rockers could get away with being average, even ugly, overweight, and boring, but Stephen had described Hudson in a way he'd never thought of himself. "Is that your reason for playing a shitload of southern rock on your radio show? I really enjoyed your run of Black Oak Arkansas the other night."

"Perhaps." The vehicle slowed. "And I'm glad you've been listening."

"Why wouldn't I? You play my fave music. You're a great deejay." Hudson set the mug in the holder. "I overheard a few kids at the nursing station saying they dig your show. Sort of like Mr. Petersson letting us in on other genres."

"When it comes to the kids' dances, I don't stray from rap, techno, or hip-hop." Stephen's lips formed into an amused smile.

"Do you enjoy playing those tunes?"

"No." Stephen shrugged. "But I have to play what they want to hear."

Hudson snickered. "Are you going to give me the *those kids can't appreciate real music* speech? Face it. We're getting old."

"C'mon. We're thirty-two. Don't put us in the senior citizens category yet." Stephen grinned.

"You got it. You're hardly a senior citizen." Hudson licked his lips. The man was in his prime—tight, sexy muscles and a gorgeous face. Most people peaked in their mid-twenties. As for Stephen, he was fine wine. Hudson had to remember he'd never met Stephen's paternal side of the family. Maybe all the Brandt men aged gracefully. Mr. Brandt sure had.

Stephen arched his black brow. "Neither are you. I told you before—you look great."

Hudson's heart pounded at Stephen, of all people, flirting. Should he come back with a sexy reply? What about their friendship he'd hoped to jumpstart?

Stephen's cheeks reddened. "I mean . . . uh, I wasn't trying to—"

Fuck it. "How great?" Hudson's skin burned hot. The man beside him wasn't the only one with a tomato-red face.

CHAPTER FIVE: WILD-EYED NORTHERN BOYS

Stephen turned his head. All traces of red faded. "Really great. I mean *really*."

"Easy to say behind sunglasses. Try taking them off and saying that again." Hudson's heart thumped. He half wanted to smack himself for following Stephen down the path, but also to cheer himself for daring to walk into the unknown, a place he'd avoided ever since he'd moved back to the reserve.

Stephen slipped off his sunglasses. "You want me to take off anything else?" He set the black frames on the dashboard. His smile matched the wicked twinkle in his blue eyes.

Hudson's mouth fell open. Heart pounding, he sputtered through god-awful spittle before his brain could scream at him not to do it, "You go ahead and take off whatever you want. Get as comfy as you like."

Stephen flashed another smile. "I'd like to. I mean I'd *really* like to, but as you can see, my hands are a little busy." He wiggled his fingers on the steering wheel. "You got two free hands, though." He winked.

Not only did Hudson's heart pound, his dick throbbed, ready to jump from his jeans. If his blood kept racing at this pace, he'd keel over. "I . . . I . . . "

The vehicle rolled to a stop. Stephen slid the gearshift into park.

Hudson straightened in his seat.

Stephen moved his hand off the steering wheel, but the

fingers of his right hand grazed the gearshift. "There. All free. Do you want me to put my hands to use on me or you?" He loosened a couple of buttons on his shirt and exposed his smooth, hard skin.

Hudson sucked in his breath. The man could always spin him into a trance, whether from a sassy smile, a saucy wink, or even vegging out in front of the TV, for cripe's sake. "Me." He leaned forward. "You."

"Maybe both?" Stephen also leaned in.

The spicy scent Hudson got a whiff of earlier tickled his nostrils. "Yeah. Both."

There wasn't anything to fear. They'd done this a million times in the past. Hudson had to keep in mind he'd made every move when Stephen had been filled with fright and doubt. He brushed his palm along Stephen's face. The lush skin teased the tips of Hudson's fingers. Only their heavy breathing and the whistling of the wind sounded through the SUV.

Stephen wrapped his fingers around Hudson's wrist. He closed his eyes.

Hudson fought for air. Stephen's lips were puckered—ready for a kiss. Just as Hudson drew another good helping of air into his lungs, Stephen joined their mouths as one.

After fifteen years, they'd sealed the rift between them.

When Stephen parted his lips, scorching heat and slick saliva invaded Hudson's mouth, stopping his heart cold. He licked at the wet tongue tangling with his. The fine hairs on the back of his neck stood at attention, and sweat formed in the pits of his arms.

Hudson slid his hand into the opening of Stephen's shirt. In the past, this was what shook him from head to toe—having Stephen responding to his touch. It wasn't any different today. Knowing Stephen wanted him—the muscles of Hudson's stomach contracted. Sticky, sizzling excitement formed in his underwear. If they kept kissing, he'd have a mess of precum in his pants, but he didn't want to stop, because Stephen's mouth was too hot and wet. Damn teasing.

The licks were a bath of pure pleasure. Only Stephen's mouth could drive Hudson batshit crazy. The taste and smell were spinning him into a spell, where submission was compulsory, not an elective. He pressed harder against Stephen's mouth, his body screaming for more.

Without having to think, he delved farther into Stephen's shirt, caressing the firm muscles. It'd been a torturous, too-long time since he'd last touched every inch of Stephen's skin. Hudson's fingers needed more flesh, and he laid his hand over Stephen's left pec. He couldn't resist toying with the nipple hardening between his thumb and index finger.

Stephen must've been feeling the same pleasure, because his palm brushed Hudson's shoulder and then trailed along his arm. The more he was explored, the greater the electrical excitement that shot through Hudson. His forearm received a silky caress, followed by his stomach, where . . .

He squirmed. Why did Stephen have to touch him there, the very spot where Hudson still had a paunch? But he didn't protest, even when his mind screamed he needed fifteen more pounds to lose if he was going to get dirty with a man who could model on men's fashion magazines.

Stephen's hand glided over Hudson's small paunch and settled beneath his belt, hidden under his pathetic mini tire.

Hudson broke the kiss.

They stared at each other. Confusion settled in Stephen's intense gaze that was potent enough to slice through Hudson's skin.

"Is . . . um . . . I guess I shouldn't have . . ." Stephen's stammering put a stutterer to shame.

"No." Hudson stiffened. "It's not you. I . . . I'm a bit sensitive about the weight I put on over the years."

The intensity in Stephen's gaze vanished and shifted to understanding. "There's nothing to be self-conscious about. I'm here, with you, am I not?"

Hudson tried to nod, but the stiffening of his neck from the tension shooting through his veins had turned him into the tin man.

"All I was doing was touching you. You don't know how bad I wanna keep touching you." Desperation was in Stephen's declaration.

His pleading dissolved the last drop of Hudson's uncertainty. "Me, too."

Stephen once again smothered Hudson's mouth. He reached for Stephen's tongue, tangling their wet flesh once more. Sure, the console was beginning to dig into Hudson, along with the seatbelt buckle, but there was room in the back for them to get comfortable.

He re-slid his fingers into Stephen's half-unbuttoned shirt. When he caressed the smooth, firm skin, his palm almost sighed. No longer did he give a shit about his paunch. If Stephen went for Hudson's belt again, he was all for an unbuckling.

The hum of an engine joined the whistling wind, their breaths heavy enough to fog up the windows if the heater wasn't running.

What the fuck? Of all the sucky timing.

Stephen broke the kiss. Through heavy lids and fighting to catch some air, he said, "I swear the white highway is busier than the Trans Canada." Frustration was reflected in his gaze.

"So the folks at the nursing station told me." Hudson eased his hand out from Stephen's shirt. He adjusted his sweater. What a bad idea to wear wool beneath his clothing. "Hot."

"Me, too."

"You're only wearing a shirt."

"I cursed my vanity at first, but I guess I shouldn't, hey?"

Stephen hit the button to lower his window just as a rusted-out truck stopped beside them.

A woman poked her round face from the vehicle. "*Boozhoo.* Everything okay?"

"We're fine. We stopped to refill our coffees. Thanks for checking."

Hudson covered his mouth to hide his grin because a helping of annoyance was in Stephen's voice, even though he smiled. The chuckle threatened to erupt into outright laughter, so Hudson bit the inside of his cheek. He was also disappointed, but Stephen's tight-set jaw indicated a very rare temper was about to erupt.

The woman said a few more things—basic chitchat of the purpose of their trip and asked why they were leaving the reserve. A couple of minutes later, she rolled up her window and waved. The man driving the truck also waved.

Stephen hit the button, and his window rose. The smile still plastered on his face, he waved. The vanishing vehicle was covered by the wake of snow its tires churned up.

Hudson finally expelled the laugh. "You don't look too happy."

Stephen arched his brow. "Are you?"

"Nope."

"Then why are you laughing?"

"You're too damn sexy when you're mad."

"I'm not mad. I understand the white highway's for everyone, and people stop to check if you're parked. The code of the road." This time Stephen's dimples appeared. "I wish they would have been assholes and blown right by us."

"Me, too." Hudson set his palm on the back of Stephen's hand resting on the gearshift. "At least you don't have blue balls."

"Blue balls." Stephen's voice carried a trace of excitement. He peered at Hudson's crotch.

Yep, that's exactly where Hudson wanted those eyes peeking. He lifted his sweater.

Stephen's gaze burned hot. "Any other time I'd suggest we shouldn't let it go to waste —"

"We are pros at the backseat." Hudson snickered and also groaned. The guy appeared ready to eat him alive. They should toss aside the duffel bags and get comfy. His softening cock began to re-stiffen.

"Tempting. But someone else will be along soon, and the next car could be one of my students. The last thing I need is my grade six class laughing about Mr. Brandt giving a blow job to Mr. Suggashie in the backseat of his SUV on the winter road. It'd be all over the rez. I'd get fired."

They laughed.

Hudson squeezed Stephen's hand. "Then you'd better hurry to Red Lake. I'm getting hard again."

"You are?" Stephen laced their fingers. He pecked Hudson's lips. "How about I check us in after I drop you off at the garage? You can stop at the pharmacy and —"

"You mean you didn't pack *those* kinds of provisions?" Hudson motioned at the backseat.

"Believe me — I thought about it." Stephen blushed. "I . . ." His gaze bobbed. "I didn't want you to think I was . . ." He cleared his throat. "I didn't want you to think I was being too bold."

"I like it when you're bold. It used to turn me on big time when you'd get bold." Hudson nuzzled Stephen's warm cheek.

"You did? You do?" Desire crackled in Stephen's voice.

"Yeah, I did, and I still do." Hudson silently offered a *thank you* for Stephen's daringness today because he'd even initiated their flirting. In the past, the poor guy had been too bashful to instigate anything between them.

He wants me. He really wants me. But . . . can I trust him?

"I guess for our next trip, I'd better make sure the

emergency bag has the right stuff?" Stephen's breath steamed Hudson's ear.

"Next trip? Sounds good to me." Hudson's heart fluttered. The thought of cancelling his room left him shaking.

"Uh, so, are—are you going to cancel your . . ." Stephen drew away. His eyes widened. "I mean, you don't have to if you don't want to."

Was this day happening, or did Hudson lie in bed dreaming? *Pinch me.* "I . . . I'll do that first thing." He touched Stephen's face.

Stephen's eyes widened. "You will?"

"Yeah."

The big smile Stephen displayed easily erased the fear somersaulting in Hudson's stomach. Maybe he could trust this guy again with his heart.

"I gotta admit . . ." Stephen's face reddened. "I'm glad you are."

"Umm . . . yeah?" Hudson exhaled the breath he'd been holding.

"Yeah." Stephen's eyes twinkled. "You saved me from . . . well, having to dig up more courage to . . ."

"You were going to ask?" The shock threading through Hudson almost made him jump.

Stephen nodded, face still red. He ducked his head. "I wasn't sure how, but by the time we had dinner I wanted to . . . umm . . ."

"I gotta admit I am digging your new boldness. Since you're used to me being bold . . ." Hudson leaned in, still shaking. Oh boy, trust was a big word, but if Stephen was asking for a second chance . . ."When I get to the hotel I wanna find you without any clothes on. In bed. Got it?"

"I will." Stephen feathered his lips against Hudson's mouth. "Turns me on knowing you want me as bad as I want you."

"Same here." Hudson still couldn't believe Stephen wanted to take another trip together. They did have a second chance. More than a chance. Endless nights. The rest-of-their-lives-together nights.

Hold up. To not repeat his past mistakes and have Stephen shove him away again, Hudson had to keep his eagerness in check by taking *them* slowly.

He could do this. He could put his heart on the line one more time. Stephen could be trusted. But Hudson's stomach muscles contracted.

Chapter Six—One Time for Old Times

Once Hudson retrieved his truck from the garage, he raced through Red Lake's only set of lights on Highway 105 to the pharmacy. Behind the building of his intended destination was Howey Bay. The small town, built much like his reserve on the water, was a beautiful site of dead-end streets and too many stop signs. After living in the city for so long, he'd forgotten how at the age of twelve he'd once considered this small community *urban* compared to where he'd grown up.

He checked the clock on the stereo. Quarter to five. If the place was closed, there'd be hell to pay. He'd almost missed the garage which had been readying to call it a day when Stephen had dropped Hudson off.

A smile spread across his face. Stephen. Waiting. Naked. In bed. Too bad there wasn't a sex shop, but with a population of four thousand—including those in Balmertown—people would order stuff online. Hudson sure wouldn't mind test driving a vibrator or butt-plug on Stephen. Adult sex easily had adolescent sex beat.

Hudson hit his turning signal and pulled into the lot. Once he parked the truck, he dashed into the still-open store.

"Hello, sir," the clerk called out. "We'll be closing in five minutes."

"No problem." Hudson stopped. "Where are your condoms and personal lubricants?"

"Third aisle." The clerk turned back to a shelf he stocked behind the counter.

Hudson scurried up the third aisle and zipped by the rows of haircare products. He halted at the condoms section, grinning. Many brands lined the two shelves. In the past, any condom had sufficed, but not tonight.

Interesting. He picked up the box. Ultra-thin for maximum sensation. Yep. Maximum sensation was what Stephen deserved. Oh boy, he wanted to give Stephen everything and have him beg for more. It seemed they'd be checking out a wee bit late tomorrow.

Hudson squatted and glanced over the various lubes. Which one should he pick—warming, intense, or couples? Stephen deserved all three. Hudson snatched the bottles. They had the whole night to try them out. To be on the safe side, he'd better grab another box of condoms. With his luck, the box he held would turn out defective.

He stood. Time to motor because his cock kept tingling. Hell, he tingled. Once he paid for everything, he jumped into his truck and drove off, keeping on Highway 105 for the ten-minute drive to the hotel. Along the way he passed the welcoming spruce trees bookending each side of him. Then he made his turn off to Highway 125.

It was a scenic drive of more spruce trees and small lakes, making the area the perfect place for fishing, camping, and every other outdoor activity—a nature lover's paradise.

He crossed the bridge of the Chukuni River, a marker telling him he was closing in on the town—and closing in on Stephen.

Hudson entered the hotel room to a cloud of steam. The sound of running water came from the bathroom. He couldn't help his big grin. Stephen must be soaping up his gorgeous body all for . . . *me*.

Almost chuckling, he tossed aside his duffel bag but kept hold of the pharmacy goodies. As he darted through the open door of the bathroom a haze of humidity hit him. His breathing accelerated. The familiar fear inched up his spine, and he squeezed his eyes shut. *Please don't let him hurt me again.*

As calmly as he could, Hudson set the bag on the vanity.

After fifteen years of believing they were kaput, he was about to — no way, not make love. His heart he'd pieced back together sure as hell wasn't ready to go *there*. After fifteen years, he'd have *sex* with the only man he'd ever wanted. There. Much better.

The shower stopped, and the curtain drew back. Stephen blinked. His smile was pure delight. "Wow, you're fast. I thought I'd have time to clean up."

"Do you mean am I disappointed you're not in bed? Nope." Hudson removed his parka, his pulse points picking up speed.

Water dripped along Stephen's chest. Beads of moisture trickled down his high cheekbones, glided along his wide shoulders, and snaked from his flat stomach to his crotch. And what a crotch. Curly pubes and soft flesh ready for some serious jerking or a cock sucking.

Hudson pulled the sweater over his head. He tossed the wool garment beside his parka on the floor. "I'm disappointed you already showered. Woulda been nice to shower together."

"We still can. Need a hand washing?" Stephen disappeared behind the curtain. The water re-started.

"Sure do." Hudson tore off the rest of his too many layers. The last time they'd shared a shower was at a hotel room in Winnipeg. Naturally, the Brandts hadn't suspected anything. They'd assumed Hudson and Stephen were best friends. No big deal if two seventeen-year-old young men bunked together.

Knees knocking and sweat soaking his armpits, Hudson lifted his leg and set his foot in the tub. To still his hammering heart, he did his best to breathe evenly, but the crazy beating refused to slow.

Fire reflected in Stephen's gaze that whispered up and down Hudson's skin, daring him to come closer, and he did.

The spray of the water caught Hudson's face and flecked his chest. He stomped down his nervousness. They'd had sex plenty of times in the past, but reminding himself of that didn't stop his teeth from clicking.

"You wanna get under the water?" Stephen shifted.

Hudson wormed around him in the snug enclosure. When his dry skin brushed Stephen's wet body, he shivered.

"You cold?" Stephen swiveled on his heel and scooped up the soap. "I can imagine, considering how chilly it is out there. Maybe I can do something about it, hey?"

If Stephen wasn't nervous, Hudson would be damned if he'd remain a shaking idiot. Water moved in uneven lines along the dips and contours of Stephen's tight muscles and glistening, bronze skin. It was a good thing Hudson had committed to a healthy diet and exercise regimen, because he was about to be washed from head to toe while under Stephen's roving gaze.

"Why don't you wet your hair?" Stephen reached out and wrapped his fingers around the two elastic bands. "We should get rid of these, hmm?"

Having his braids unbound was so intimate. Kokum had said the one who first unwrapped Hudson's hair was the person meant for him. Warmth gathered at the bottom of his spine because Stephen had even done this task in their youth.

"Something I overlooked." Hudson settled under the hot spray. "Guess I was a bit eager."

"Eager?" Stephen kept unwinding Hudson's braids. "You're not the only eager beaver." He puckered his lips, his breath heating Hudson's mouth.

Hudson easily reached for the kiss. The electrifying excitement of their lips molding as one crackled through his veins. When he pressed against Stephen, their cocks and stomachs touched. Hudson slid his tongue between Stephen's parted lips. The familiar essence was pure heaven, coaxing him to plunge deep, suckle and lick every inch of the heat-filled mouth he tasted.

Stephen moaned.

Having the groan deep in Hudson's mouth seduced him to mold against Stephen's rock-hard form. He wiggled his cock along the thatch of curly hair joining with his while trailing his fingers over the rounded contour of Stephen's ass. Tight and smooth. Hudson couldn't help moving his palms in a circular motion on each cheek.

He kept sampling Stephen's mouth, whose precum moistened Hudson's belly, or maybe it was the water? Who knew and who cared. What mattered was he was exciting Stephen, his erection pushing on Hudson's gut.

He broke their kiss. "I never thought this would happen again. I expected . . ."

"Me, too." Stephen's lips caressed Hudson's jawline. "I waited so long I don't wanna talk. I want you. We can talk later."

"Why'd you take forever to start coming around the nursing station?" Hudson licked at Stephen's lobe.

Stephen softly chuckled. "I wasn't sure if you'd tell me to get lost." His suckling lips teased Hudson's throat. "I couldn't stay away, though. It was driving me batshit crazy. You were driving me batshit crazy."

Blood raced to Hudson's fingers and toes. Forget the foreplay. They had all night to explore. "Let's—Let's hurry and get outta here. I want you on the bed."

Did he ever. He ached to see Stephen flat on his back, legs

spread, waiting for a good, hard fucking.

"Same here. It's been way too long." Stephen's wet lashes fluttered.

Too long? Had Stephen been saving himself since Hudson's arrival in September? There'd been no sneaking off to the gay bars during trips into Thunder Bay or Winnipeg, as he'd assumed?

"Oh? It's my cock you were waiting for?" Hudson grunted.

Stephen smiled. "You betcha." He squirted out a helping of the two-in-one shampoo.

Hudson closed his eyes. His shoulders loosened, but his cock remained hard. The massaging of his scalp was plush enough to kiss the most sensitive spots on his body—sorta like Stephen's voice. Hudson eased under the spray and washed out the shampoo. Before he opened his eyes, Stephen's firm, smooth hands melted against his flesh and worked the soap along his skin.

Hudson grinned while being scrubbed from top to bottom. Each swipe of the soap and gentle touch from Stephen's hand left Hudson's stomach somersaulting. When Stephen's palm cupped Hudson's balls, his breathing jumped. That spot better be off limits for now or he'd come.

He gripped Stephen's wrist. "Better let me wash it. If you do . . . I'll ruin it for us."

"You think so?" Stephen snickered and straightened.

Hudson worked the soap into his crotch. "Yeah. I want you too bad."

"How about I let you finish up then? I'll meet you in the bedroom." Stephen stepped away.

"Sounds like a plan." Hudson rinsed off. "The lube and condoms are in the pharmacy bag."

"Go ahead and use my stuff. I don't want you taking too long with unpacking." Stephen vanished from the tub.

Hudson did as suggested and raced through his routine of

shaving, brushing his teeth, flossing, and slathering on a helping of deodorant. Five minutes later, he left the bathroom. He held a towel, squeezing the excess water from his hair.

Stephen lay stretched out on the bed, elbow pressed into the mattress and his hand offering support for his head. His cock was hard, and fine hairs flecked his long legs crossed at the ankles. His smile was big enough to light his eyes.

The saliva in Hudson's mouth drained away.

Stephen moved his index finger in a circular motion. His grin was as playful as his wolfish, twinkling gaze.

"Y'know that look always got under my skin?" Hudson rested his hand against the dresser. "You used to do that in the past."

"The past?" Stephen patted the bed. "You got it. One time for old times, eh?" He chuckled.

Hudson stiffened. The invitation was no longer teasing but a slap in the face. If that wasn't a crock of bullshit nerve, he didn't know what was. The guy was daring to treat this as a joke? A *let's get in the sack and play out the past*?

He'd been right not to trust Stephen.

Hudson tossed the towel over the chair and eased onto the bed, even when his brain chastised him for allowing himself to be used. "Sorry. Had to brush my teeth and stuff," he mumbled.

"You're shaking." Stephen clutched Hudson's fingers.

Damn straight I'm shaking. Why else would I shake? Hudson leaned in and pressed his lips against Stephen's. It was best not to talk, or Lord knew what would leave Hudson's mouth, because his gut continued to twist. Raw heat scorched the back of his neck. The blood pumping through his veins demanded he break Stephen's fingers. Instead, Hudson stroked them.

He must calm down and keep his emotions in check, but how could he? By default, Hudson had won his way into

Stephen's bed, seeing how there was no other gay man on the reserve but him, so of course he'd been invited to enjoy *one time for old times.*

Stephen broke the kiss. "What's wrong?"

"Nothing." Again, Hudson pressed his lips against Stephen's mouth. They'd share a fuck and not a dime more.

You want sex but not my love. I'll give you sex. The kind of sex a selfish jerk deserves.

Again, Stephen broke the kiss. "No. Something's wrong."

Hot coals burned Hudson's gut. He grunted. "I see. It's gotta be your way—like always."

"What do you mean?" Stephen shifted.

"What do you think I mean?" Hudson also shifted. He was too good to be the default guy.

"I don't know. I'm not a mind reader." Confusion surfaced in Stephen's eyes.

"This isn't rocket science." Hudson jumped off the bed. "How do you think I felt after you probably unzipped your pants for anyone who asked, but I had to spend two goddamn years begging?"

He stormed for the door where he'd left his duffel bag.

The bed creaked. "I see." Stephen's voice was quiet.

Leave it to Stephen to have no other words to say. And he'd probably let Hudson leave without a fight, too.

Good riddance. Hudson snatched a fresh pair of jeans from the duffel bag. Forget the long underwear. It'd take forever to dress when his pride demanded he make a quick exit.

The bed creaked again. Footsteps padded along the worn carpet. Stephen appeared in Hudson's peripheral vision. He growled at the sight of the long legs he'd used to caress, full balls he'd sucked, and the soft cock he'd teased into many erections.

Damn the sight of Stephen thrashing and grinding beneath Hudson while moans had filled his ears. He squeezed his lids shut.

June third. Stephen's seventeenth birthday. Hudson had given the guy he'd loved the finest rim and blow job a man could ask for. The next day during their evening fish, Stephen had refused to keep his shorts on. They went beyond oral and made themselves one on the floor of old Stan's tackle shack. The Brandts had questioned the lack of walleye Hudson and Stephen had failed to catch afterward, because they'd spent the remainder of the summer screwing instead of casting their lines into the water.

Hudson opened his eyes. It seemed Stephen still couldn't get enough of sex. *You can't even put on a robe while you confront me.* "I should've expected this. Being the only other gay man on the rez."

Stephen's mouth fell open as if he'd been slapped. "You-You really believe I . . ." His pain-filled gaze darted about.

"What else am I supposed to believe?" Hudson tugged the sweater over his head. He pulled on the hem.

"Th-that we were friends. Best friends." Stephen's voice crackled.

"Friends? Seems you only remember us as friends." Hudson donned a fresh pair of socks. "That's all you ever talk about."

Stephen's Adam's apple bobbed. "True. I didn't want to bring it up because I wasn't sure how you'd react, but I guess I can mention it now since you did. And lovers."

"Lovers?" Hudson snorted. He donned the other sock. "Lovers means two people in love. You keep forgetting that I loved you but you didn't feel the same way. After I *finally* got you to trust me, all you wanted was sex. And nothing's changed 'cause all you still want is sex from me."

"What?" Stephen gasped. His big eyes widened. "I did not. I do not. How can you say that?"

Hudson stomped into the bathroom. He snatched his boots and parka off the floor. As he stormed to the entranceway, he

51

tugged on the big, heavy coat.

"What else am I supposed to believe? I told you I loved you and you kicked my balls. But I bet your other men sure didn't get kicked in the balls when they said those three dumb words. Nice. Real nice."

He yanked on his bootlaces. "Go on and fuck a hole in the wall 'cause you're not seeing anything from me. I need something else. I had sex for fifteen years with four different men, and it got me nowhere. So excuse me while I book a flight to Winnipeg for next weekend. Maybe I'll find someone who isn't afraid of *my* love."

He slung the duffel bag strap over his shoulder and yanked open the door. All he had to do was leave, but his pounding heart he loathed yearned for Stephen to stop him. The coward wouldn't because he hadn't in the past.

Chest heavy, Hudson slammed the door to the hotel room. Just as expected, Stephen let fifteen years ago repeat itself.

CHAPTER SEVEN: CAN'T KEEP A GOOD MAN DOWN

This was a nightmare — a repeat of fifteen years ago.

Stephen shook his head. *You're not at the dock and you're not a cowardly seventeen-year-old punk who's afraid of what Dad and everyone else will say. Get your tail out from between your legs and go after him.*

He darted into the bathroom and snatched his bathrobe off the hook. Holy Moses, he never knew what to make of Hudson. Yes, his anger had been justified in the past, but as for today, Stephen had assumed they'd settled everything.

Maybe his offer to help retrieve the truck, playing *Back Where You Belong* on his radio show, and what they'd shared while traveling to Red Lake had missed the mark? One thing about Hudson Suggashie — he always shot first and asked questions later.

Spell it out. He wants to hear that you love him.

"Wait!" Stephen couldn't get his arms into the sleeves of the robe because he moved too fast. "For fuck sakes." He finally wormed his way into the useless garment and tied the belt.

When he flung open the door, he gaped at an empty hallway.

Sweet Jesus, Hudson couldn't get away fast enough. He must have run for the stairs. Where did he go, and would he come back?

Stephen swallowed. The last fight they'd had, Hudson had hopped a plane and bolted for Winnipeg. What if he'd fled for the reserve to pack and leave again? Stephen darted for the stairs since there wasn't an elevator. But Hudson wasn't on the staircase either. Maybe he was getting a room? Stephen popped out in the main hallway and dashed for the front desk a few meters away.

The clerk removed his glasses. He held his nose in the air. "Can I help you?"

"Yes." Panting, Stephen blurted out, "Did Hudson Suggashie check in?"

The clerk slowly looked Stephen up and down. "I can't give you information about guests—especially someone who isn't wearing any clothes."

Not a hint of heat flecked Stephen's cheeks. This was an emergency. "Then can you ring his room, please?"

The clerk folded his arms. "There's no room to ring."

Stephen's heart crashed to the worn rug. Hudson had bolted for the reserve. This was a nightmare—a repeat of fifteen years ago, and Stephen hadn't seen Hudson for fifteen years after he'd boarded that plane.

The pain throbbing in Stephen's temples wasn't from being punched in the heart by Hudson. Responsible for his headache was the wine he'd bought last night at the liquor store to drown his misery after retiring to his hotel room. Making the drive back to the reserve early in the morning had been torture while hungover. Scratch that. Hungover and plain miserable about how everything had blown up in his face.

At least the landing to the community was up ahead. All he had left to do was crawl into bed and pretend yesterday never happened. With the radio on low, he cruised through the Sawbuck district first. Since the temperature had lowered to minus thirty-eight Celsius, nobody was around.

Gassing up his SUV could wait until tomorrow. He checked the fuel gauge. The cranked heater had left the tank low. When he hit Main, a part of the reserve he had to pass to get to Seven Mile, he couldn't control his gaze from traveling to Hudson's house. Light came from the living room window facing the road. A truck Stephen wasn't familiar with, but most likely belonging to Hudson, was parked in the driveway.

Stephen let his foot off the gas pedal. At one-thirty in the afternoon, the curtains were wide open. He kept creeping by the house. The back door opened. Just as Hudson stepped outside, probably to get more firewood, Stephen slammed on the gas pedal to get the hell out of there. But he gave too much punch, and the tires to the SUV spun on the ice, leaving him sitting in the middle of the road.

Hudson glanced over his shoulder, most likely wondering what fool didn't know how to winter drive.

Heat grew beneath Stephen's skin. He eased his foot on the pedal to get the vehicle moving at a delicate pace to drive off on glare ice. Even worse, he met Hudson's angry stare. Before Stephen made a safe getaway, his peripheral vision caught Hudson's frown.

Stephen whacked the steering wheel. Dammit, he'd blown it. Once Hudson got into that kind of mood, there was no changing his mind. For the second time, Stephen had lost the man he loved . . . forever.

Like the fool he was, Hudson jogged around to the front of the house. He managed to catch the back end of the SUV disappearing down the road, heading for Seven Mile. His pulse points wouldn't stop fluttering. Although he knew he'd done the right thing by leaving Balmertown yesterday evening, his cracked heart kept telling him no surgeon could repair what was broken. The only fix was Stephen.

There was firewood to gather for his stove. Stew to start for his supper. Ham to throw in the oven. He folded his arms and trudged back around the side of the house to the woodpile. At least Stephen had someone to go home to—his mother. As for Hudson, it'd be another quiet evening alone.

Fine, he wanted one time for old times . . . *can I do it? Can I simply sleep with him?* Being alone was making Hudson more bitter than The Grinch stealing everyone's Christmas. His original plan to remain friends and only friends wasn't working, because his dick was telling him otherwise. As for trusting Stephen, that was a big fat no. Never again would he trust the likes of Stephen Brandt.

Still, Hudson's cock was deathly lonesome. And if Stephen wanted *one time for old times,* he'd get more than that. He'd get sex and only sex. By the time Hudson was finished, Stephen would feel as used as Hudson had.

He gathered up the firewood and stomped back inside. The landline sat on the kitchen counter, daring him to pick it up and make the call.

Hudson squared his shoulders, dumped the firewood next to the woodstove, and removed his parka. He strode straight for the telephone and snatched up the cordless receiver because the cell phone tower was out of service again. The great perks of living up north. Before he could chicken out or second-guess himself, he punched in the numbers to Stephen's place he knew by heart since Mrs. Brandt was his patient at the nursing station.

On three rings, Mrs. Brandt's familiar voice came through.

"Hello, Mrs. Brandt. It's Hudson Suggashie. Is Stephen there?"

"Oh, Hudson. I thought he was helping you retrieve your truck?" Puzzlement filled her soft voice. "Wait a second. He just pulled up. Did you two get your truck?"

"Yes. We got it yesterday. I don't have to ask for rides to the nursing station anymore."

"Wonderful." But uncertainty was in her reply. "Oh, here he is. Stephen. Telephone. It's Hudson."

Hudson puffed out three quick breaths. He clutched the receiver tighter. "Stephen?"

"Uh . . . yes?" Confusion floated over the telephone wire.

"Dinner. My place. Tomorrow after work. Say . . . five-thirty?" Hudson kept squeezing the receiver.

"Oh . . . uh . . . okay."

"Great. Bye." Hudson switched off the phone and sank to his haunches, leaning against the kitchen cupboard. He rested the back of his head on the counter's edge.

He had food to buy and cleaning to do. His top priority was sexing up this place. Finally, Mr. Perfect Teeth, Perfect Smile, Perfect Body, and Perfect Hair would experience pain, humiliation, and heartbreak. Well, maybe not heartbreak. A guy needed a heart for it to break, and Stephen had proved even after fifteen years, he didn't have one.

"I won't be around for supper tomorrow night." Stephen still wore his parka and had yet to remove his boots.

Mom folded her arms. Her once black hair was now flecked with strands of gray that she kept short and clipped over her ears. "I take it you're going to eat with Hudson?"

Stephen nodded. He swiveled on his heel to grab his suitcase from the utility room.

"How did your trip go?"

"Good." *Then rotten.* Before he reached for the suitcase handle, he stopped. Something strange was going on. It wasn't like Hudson to do an about-face, and he sure wasn't the kind of guy to forgive and forget. Not from what Stephen recalled. In the past, whenever they'd argued, he'd have to coax Hudson out of a pique.

"You don't look sure of yourself." Mom turned back to the

oven. She stirred the soup in the pot that scented the kitchen.

Stephen slung the strap over his shoulder. He crossed the living room, beelining for his bedroom that was on the other end of the house from the utility room and Mom's bedroom. "I'm fine."

He shut the door. All had been going well until they'd been about to get busy on the bed after Hudson had stepped from the shower. A hundred times Stephen had played out the reason for Hudson's anger at the Balmertown Inn. Now he wanted to have supper together?

A knot formed in Stephen's stomach. Something told him to be on his guard, even call back and decline the offer, but his heart wouldn't let him. He'd best unpack and get his ass in gear because he still had to check with Jesse on how the broadcast had gone last night, since the teenager had filled in for Stephen's radio show.

One thing Hudson had to accept while living up north again was the jacked-up prices. In the past, Kokum had bought the groceries, and being a typical teenager, Hudson hadn't paid attention to what the weekly food had cost.

Even though he made a nice paycheck, he'd winced at the money he'd had to fork over for two rib eye steaks he was going to broil in the oven. The same for the Caesar salad he'd toss, and the fresh potatoes. As for the sour cream, it'd screamed eight dollars. Although the general store offered more than food, such as clothing and furniture, he'd rather pay the shipping cost to get bigger items sent up on the plane than pay the outrageous prices. Better yet, he'd haul the stuff in the winter using his truck.

He stood in front of the bathroom mirror. Tonight was the night. Already he'd set the table and had lit two candles to create a romantic ambience. The woodstove was stoked. Not too hot and not too cold. The last thing he wanted was Stephen overheating. Sure, overheating was nice, but not the wrong kind.

He'd put the offer on the table and see if Stephen agreed or not.

One time for old times, you say? I'll give you more than one time for old times.

Hudson tromped into the main bedroom and donned the jeans, collared shirt, and comfy moccasins he'd selected. As for his underwear, no need to put them on. He'd be taking them off in record time.

Fifteen minutes later, he had everything prepped. Too bad the reserve was dry. A bottle of wine would have capped off the dinner perfectly.

Headlights appeared in the living room window across the way where Hudson stood, checking the steaks he had broiling in the oven, after letting them marinate all day in the sauce he'd made. Just as the headlights vanished, his stomach tightened.

Taking in a deep breath, he strode to the back door where footsteps crunching on the steps filtered inside.

A knock.

Hudson's breathing refused to cooperate. If he didn't get his shit together, he'd pass out. He was in control now. Not Stephen. Hudson opened the door. At the sight before him, his queasy stomach almost tumbled to the floor.

The outside light revealed a lake-color blue shirt that matched Stephen's eyes. His black hair feathered his oval-shaped jawline, elongating his already high cheekbones. Instead of a parka, he'd chosen to freeze in a button-down, black leather commuter jacket that covered his thighs. His gloved long fingers clutched the strap of a paper bag.

When Stephen flashed his dimples, Hudson's scheme vanished from the recesses of his mind. All he could do was sputter. He opened the door wider. "C'mon in."

"Thanks." Stephen cleared his throat. "I brought you something." He held out the bag. "It's not wine, but I thought sparkling cider would go perfect with the meal."

Hudson reached for the offered bag. "Uh . . . oh . . . err . . . take off your . . ." *clothes.* "Take off your jacket."

Stephen removed the stylish coat and scarf to reveal his sexy V-shaped physique. A couple of buttons were undone on his shirt, offering a glimpse of his bronzed chest Hudson had stroked yesterday.

Fumbling with the bag, Hudson motioned at the dress boots Stephen wore. "Go ahead. Make yourself comfy."

Hudson stumbled for the kitchen counter, holding the bag against his chest since he didn't trust his shaking hands. He was supposed to seduce Stephen tonight?

Fuck, who was seducing who?

Chapter Eight: What Can I Do?

A s Stephen bent down to untie his boots, he couldn't help watching Hudson stride into the kitchen. The jeans offered a pleasant view of his round tush, the denim material not too tight and not too loose. Since the woodstove was casting a good helping of heat, Stephen silently patted himself on the back for being smart to wear a linen shirt instead of a bulky sweater

"Make yourself comfy," Hudson called out. He stood at the counter, chopping something.

Stephen eased from the utility room. To his left was the main bedroom, but the door was closed. He again eyed the door. Having been in this house many times in the past, he knew the bedroom was only able to accommodate a queen-size bed and a dresser.

"Why don't you open the cider?" Hudson set aside the knife and reached for the romaine lettuce. He pitched the leaves into a wooden bowl.

"Sure." There was nothing fancy to the cider. Stephen had to simply unscrew the cap. One thing about the general store, every item cost an arm or a leg. He'd had to fork out good money for the dinner gift. But Hudson was worth every penny.

Still, Stephen's knees started knocking. The suspicion that had hounded him to Main ghosted the back of his neck. For Hudson to be this friendly meant something was up.

Stephen filled the two glasses. Maybe he should stop being suspicious. The dinner could be Hudson's way of saying he'd made a mistake at the hotel in Balmertown.

Stephen sat at the dining table in the eat-in kitchen, glancing around.

The living room and kitchen remained the same. The homemade quilt with the two turtles covered the couch, a precious item Hudson's grandmother had worked tirelessly on in the quilting circle at the senior's center. A crocheted afghan draped the armchair. Mrs. Suggashie had even fashioned cushion coverings for the old rocking chair she'd knitted in while creaking back and forth in front of the woodstove. The old woman had even supported the local artists, using her pension money to purchase original paintings that hung on the walls of stained pine. Like Mom, Hudson's grandmother had preferred carpet to warm her feet during the cold mornings when the fire had burned down and the woodstove needed refueling.

Their houses were replicas, coming from the same package the reserve had purchased during one of its building projects. Hudson's former bedroom was in the same spot as Stephen's, hidden around the corner by the wall of the kitchen.

"Who's covering for you tonight?" Hudson was busy pouring dressing over the salad that must've contained bacon because the aroma filled the house.

"Jesse. He really wants to become a deejay. Radio. A big city station."

"Too bad you can't run yours full time." Hudson tossed the salad.

"I wish I could, but I only have Jesse to cover for me. Plus, running an all-day station is a full-time job." Stephen couldn't help the wistfulness in his voice.

Hudson set aside the tongs. He leaned his butt against the counter and folded his arms. "You were lying to me."

"Lying?" Stephen couldn't help his sputter. Oh boy, he had guessed correctly. Hudson was up to his usual tricks and moving in for the kill.

"About being happy you acquired your B.Ed. You never wanted to be a teacher. You want to deejay." There wasn't any guessing in Hudson's statement.

Heat crawled across Stephen's face. He shrugged. "It is what it is. There's nothing I can do about it now. Mom's disability brings in only so much money. Someone's got to pay the bills."

Hudson's dark eyes narrowed. He glanced to the sink, nodding.

Now what was going on in his devious mind? Stephen had a good hunch, like blasting him again in the same manner Hudson had done inside the hotel room.

"Yeah. I guess." Hudson opened the oven. "The potatoes are ready. And the steaks are finished."

Stephen couldn't help admiring the view of Hudson's butt once more while he moved the steaks from the broiling pan to the plates. Hunger was growing, but not for rib eye.

While Hudson set the plates on the table, Stephen continued glancing around to keep his eyes busy so his staring wouldn't get him into trouble, but he couldn't help peeking at Hudson's super-thick unbound hair falling down his back, or the choker wrapping his sturdy throat, and the denim shirt enhancing his reddish skin.

Stephen faced the sink, and the fire roared in the woodstove behind him in the living room. The window above the sink gave a view of the pitch-black blanketing the backyard.

"All ready. *Ambe daga wiisinidaa.*" Hudson grinned. The smile plumped up his chubby cheeks that were handsome on him.

Although far from fluent in *Anishinaabemowin,* Stephen had heard enough Ojibway spoken over the years and at special feasts to understand Hudson had said *come on, let's eat.*

"It smells great. You outdid yourself." Stephen picked up

his knife and fork. The delicious scent of the marinade coming from the steak was inviting him to dive in.

"Thanks. Specially made for you." Hudson grinned and winked.

Stephen stiffened. He'd never witnessed Hudson winking before. Was the meal poisoned? He sniffed, but no strange odor came from the delicious meat on his plate. He cut the rib eye into bite-sized pieces and sampled the steak that was tender enough to melt on his tongue. But trying to chew was impossible, no matter how succulent the piece in his mouth. The feeling was reminiscent of opening a closet door to the deep darkness of the unknown. He could almost see the mischief surrounding Hudson, and not the cute devilish kind either, but pure malice.

"Can I ask you something?" Stephen reached for the glass to wash down the steak that refused to be swallowed.

"Sure." Hudson also reached for his glass, but since his words hadn't carried a mouthful of food, he'd managed to swallow, Stephen noted.

At least one of them was at ease, and Hudson was because he had a plan in motion. Stephen wasn't born yesterday. He knew this man too well.

"May I ask something?" Stephen took a big gulp of the cider.

"Sure." Hudson kept stuffing his face.

Stephen had forgotten how much Hudson enjoyed a delicious meal, and when perturbed, turned to food to calm his nerves. "What did I say to upset you in the hotel room? Can you please level with me? I thought we were being pretty honest with each other."

Hudson shrugged and kept eating. "We'll talk after the meal. Sound good?"

What choice did Stephen have? He nodded.

For the rest of dinner, while Hudson merrily ate, Stephen

had to force down his steak, salad, and baked potato. The unsufferable silence was also too much for his ears. By the time he swallowed the last piece of meat, he'd drunk two glasses of cider to get the food down. Too bad there wasn't alcohol in the bottle. Scratch that. He'd drunk enough wine in the hotel room.

Stephen made sure to eat everything on his plate. Hudson was as traditional as they came, and to leave even a crumb was an insult.

"Thank you. That was good." Stephen wiped his mouth and set aside his napkin. He reached for more cider and poured his third glass.

"Glad you enjoyed it." Hudson stood and beelined for the woodstove.

Stephen craned his neck toward the living room. "The question I asked earlier . . ."

"Yeah, the question." Hudson squatted. He opened the glass door and added some ash to the woodstove. "Y'know, I gotta admit you were right the first time."

"Right?" Stephen turned his chair around while Hudson used a poker to adjust the logs in the fire.

"About love. You told me we were too young . . ."

"I was wrong," Stephen quickly said.

"No. You were right." Hudson glanced over his shoulder. "We were seventeen. Who knows what love is at that age? And who needs love?" He shrugged. "I only came back because I couldn't stand the thought of anyone living in Kokum's house. Or selling it. But you gotta admit, a man has needs."

"I guess so." Stephen smoothed his palms on his thighs.

"I have a contract for two years at the nursing station. After that . . . well, we'll see . . ." Hudson kept poking at the fire.

"The move isn't permanent?" Stephen tugged at his shirt collar. He'd assumed wrong.

"I dunno. Like I said—I'll see how the job pans out. Y'know, after I messed up my other relationships, I thought to myself, love is something I'm beginning to understand I'm not good at."

Stephen's eyes widened. Hudson had been more than good at love. *He loved me with all his heart.* "I think . . . well, I think you're wrong, if you don't mind me saying."

"I don't mind." Hudson closed the door to the woodstove. He meandered over to the table. "But I failed a few times, so I think I'm better off . . . I'm gonna be honest. At this time in my life, I'm after hookups and nothing more." He sat in the chair he'd previously occupied.

Hudson's dead-eyed stare was powerful enough to almost crush Stephen's fingers. "You don't want anything other than sex?"

"That's why I asked you about hookups in the city. Bars. Those kinds of places." Hudson reached for the bottle of cider.

"But I thought we settled this?" Enough of dancing around the conversation. Stephen lifted his chin in determination and placed his hands on the table. "I apologized. I said I was wrong. I was a coward who should've found my balls to live my own life instead of listening to my dad. But I was scared at the time. Terrified of what he'd say."

"Is that why you suggested *one time for old times?*" Hudson's eyes narrowed.

"What?" Stephen gasped. "Is that what this is about? Did you really think I was after a one-nighter? The song by .38 Special. *One Time for Old Times.* That's why I jokingly said that. I thought you'd get the joke, but I see you're way off target."

Hudson stiffened. He glanced away, nibbling on his lower lip. Then he glanced back. "You know how the saying goes— fool me once, shame on you. Fool me twice, shame on me."

Stephen couldn't believe what he was hearing. *He really*

believes I'm after sex. He doesn't believe I really loved him. He sank in the chair, close to putting his hands over his face, but he kept them on the table. Could he blame Hudson, though? The poor guy had opened his heart and received a kick to the balls.

If they were going to move forward, Stephen would have to prove his love. If that meant having to take whatever Hudson dished out, Stephen would do it. He stared at his lap. "You said you want to go into the city for hookups."

"Yeah."

Stephen kept staring at his lap. The jealousy gnawed at him. If Hudson wanted a no-strings night of sex, then . . .

Before he could contemplate the consequences, the words rushed from Stephen's mouth. "I'm a gay man. Why not me? Judging by your . . . reaction to me in Red Lake, I'd say we still share an attraction."

Hudson's eyes narrowed. "Yes, an attraction."

"I, however, wish there could be more," Stephen added in a small voice, "but you're being quite clear about what you want."

The glower vanished from Hudson's eyes, and they became softer. He picked up the glass and swirled the contents. "I guess this is *one time for old times*. Or maybe two times for old times. Or three times for old times."

Stephen sank in the chair. "I guess . . . I guess it is."

The temptation to tuck his tail between his legs and slink from the house clawed at Stephen, but he remained in his chair. Somehow, he'd find a way for them to recapture what they'd once had, but how long he could hold out being used for sex, he wasn't sure.

"Are we starting tonight?"

"There's no time like the present, is there?" The smile Hudson bared was a smirk, hardly warm.

CHAPTER NINE: BONE AGAINST STEEL

Hudson remained at the kitchen table. He made no move to get up and locked his thick fingers around the buttons of his shirt. Slowly, he undid each one.

Stephen's brain screamed at him to get the hell out while he stood a chance, but his heart kept him parked in the kitchen chair. Why couldn't he possess the temper and vindictiveness of Hudson?

Even though fear rattled Stephen's teeth, he couldn't tear his gaze from the bronzed chest being bared for him. Finally, what he longed for was about to happen, not on the terms he'd hoped for, but it was a start. If he could hold out long enough, maybe there was the chance he could have Hudson's love once again.

If they were starting the *no-strings attached* tonight, Stephen had best reach for his own buttons. As he regretfully unfastened them, Hudson's stare, full of hunger, capable of eating Stephen alive, shook him to his core. While continuing to shiver, he let the garment fall to the floor. Sure, they'd gotten naked many times, even at the hotel, but baring himself for Hudson at the dinner table was Stephen losing his virginity again. He was a teenager, daring to taste the forbidden.

Hudson cast aside his shirt, displaying his bronze skin. He raised his chin in a defiant sort of way, as if daring Stephen to find fault with his physique. There was not an imperfection to be spied on Hudson's smooth chest and rounded belly that Stephen yearned to touch.

Hudson clamped his fingers around his belt buckle and

unfastened the snap.

The beating of Stephen's heart was vinyl spinning on a turntable faster than thirty-three rpms. He was about to spin right off the record player and hit the wall at full force. Following Hudson's lead, Stephen also worked his belt open, even though he wished they could undress each other, but perhaps intimacy wasn't allowed during hookups? It wasn't like he'd gone cruising when he'd lived in southern Ontario. Even though he knew he'd be used merely for sex, his cock strained against his pants, ready to jump from his underwear.

With a still-blank stare, Hudson lowered the zipper to his jeans.

Stephen licked his lips at what he'd devoured and even touched at the Balmertown Inn. Even better, there was no underwear hiding what his mouth begged to feast on. First the shiny head slick with precum was revealed for his viewing pleasure. Then inch by inch, the thick girth and length dared him to wrap his hands around Hudson's dick and jerk him into submission. Tight balls full of jizz were bait for Stephen to lick and get sucked into the net with no escape.

"I showed you mine. Let's see yours." The flatness of Hudson's tone didn't match the excitement of his proud erection.

Stephen stood and lowered his zipper. As he touched the waist of his own pants to free his cock from his underwear, his breathing intensified.

"Why'd you bother to wear them?" Hudson's gaze stroked Stephen's boner. "You knew what would happen after dinner."

"Honestly," Stephen choked out, "I wasn't sure what to expect."

"Whenever you come here, expect to get your schlong blown." The grin Hudson flashed was as wicked as the glint in his eyes that possessed small lids and were wider than they were round. "I wanna suck it. You got the hottest prick I ever saw."

Stephen was midway through working his pants off and stopped. The declaration went straight to the head of his cock, as if Hudson had swirled his tongue around the sensitive tip. "Yours isn't a slouch either."

Hudson rounded the table, thick thighs brushing one another. His erection bounced against his lower abs, and his stare wasn't on Stephen but his cock.

Stephen stiffened. He braced his hands on the back of the chair.

"Allow me." Hudson shifted to his knees.

The excitement coursing through Stephen's veins was a flash of lightning streaking through the sky. He held his breath, staring down at Hudson's mouth a sniff away from his throbbing tip, anticipating sliding into wet, silky flesh.

Hudson's hands glided along Stephen's hips, leaving a trail of heat on his skin. When Stephen's ass was cupped, the warmth from Hudson's palms almost melted him into a puddle. He thrust and was drawn between Hudson's lips, the softest and most delicious mouth he'd ever fucked.

His cock was feasted on with succulent licks that tasted every inch of his length and were bestowed on the tip of his erection. The teasing was so unbearable, Stephen couldn't help holding Hudson by the back of the head to shove his cock faster and quicker into the hot depths that wrapped his dick like a second skin. The exquisiteness of being enveloped in such wet pleasure left his head spinning.

Being sucked off was drawing forth the familiar pleasure from when Stephen had beaten off in the shower, but this time his cum wasn't going to waste. It'd be swallowed by the man he wanted.

Stephen pressed both hands on the back of Hudson's head to feed him every inch he possessed. He fucked hard and fast, the release creeping up behind him, ready to capture him in the heady sensations. The tip of his cock pulsated as the explosion swept him into euphoria. He groaned and cried out. A million jolts of electricity flickered through his body and then shot through him, blasting his thick jizz into Hudson's mouth.

Stephen stiffened, reveling in the heady bliss that had taken his breath away. His panting was fast and heavy. He gasped, still marveling from the sensational pleasure he'd received from Hudson's mouth that were tiny aftershocks pinging through Stephen's limbs.

Hudson flicked at the tip of Stephen's dick, and he shuddered. His erection was being released, Hudson's mouth sliding along Stephen's length.

Stephen set his hands on the back of the chair, staring down at Hudson, who gazed up, the expression familiar—a star-struck teenager gaping in amazement at him. He couldn't help but glide his fingers through the thick strands of Hudson's hair, who gave one last lick before allowing Stephen to completely free his dick. Another spasm quaked through him, and he juddered.

Hudson's tongue snaked out and captured a dollop of cum attempting to slip from the corner of his mouth. The same hunger that had appeared over dinner was back in his black eyes. Gone was the gaping teenager. He slowly rose, and as he stood, his palms skimmed the sides of Stephen's body. The caressing left tiny electrical currents on his skin.

Before he could blink or question Hudson, Stephen was spun around, forced to face the utility room door and the master bedroom adjacent to it. The sound of a drawer opening and closing piqued his curiosity.

"Spread 'em," Hudson ordered, his voice a mixture between a command and desperation.

Stephen spread his legs. The middle of his back, right in the sweet spot of his spine, received a tender kiss that left his thighs quivering, close to giving out on him. Hudson continued planting tender kisses on each bump of Stephen's spine. Stephen gripped the chair tighter since he was being coaxed into submitting. His head lolled to the side, and the last of the tension in his shoulders vanished. Each pucker was like being rolled into a vat of cotton balls.

Hudson didn't stop until he reached the cleft of Stephen's ass. The sensitive spot received a sweet kiss and tongue bath. Stephen gasped and stared down at the front of the chair.

His cheeks were spread, and Hudson kept planting sweet kisses on Stephen's cleft. Then each buttock received a peck gratifying enough to stir his soft dick that he'd thought was drained of all cum.

Hudson's kisses moved lower. The warm air from the fire in the woodstove whispered along Stephen's exposed hole, but just as quickly was snuffed out when Hudson's mouth melted against the opening.

Having his asshole teased with such a delicate kiss drained the air from Stephen's lungs. He almost collapsed from the compliance his body was undergoing. Forcing himself to grip the chair tighter, he dug his fingers in, but trying to remain tense was difficult when his crack was being bathed with Hudson's gentle puffs of warm breath.

When the tip of Hudson's tongue touched Stephen's bare crack, the tension that had washed away the heat from the fire returned at full force. His once soft spine became tauter than one of the many icicles hanging on the eavestroughs on Hudson's house. The budding anticipation was growing in Stephen's crotch, a maddening game of waiting and wishing for an ass eating.

Slowly, Hudson drew his tongue down the vulnerable line between Stephen's buttocks. He was being hit with a million jolts of high voltage. His body screamed, and a loud groan flew from his mouth. His chin hit his chest and he licked his lips, his body stiff and wondering when the sexual attack would commence.

But Hudson chose to bestow his attention on the area between Stephen's balls and asshole—the sweet spot that always made him groan and moan. He thrust his ass out, grinding his hips, working his asshole toward Hudson's mouth. Finally, his opening received a kiss. Not just any kiss. A French kiss taunting his insides with hot licks and plenty of spit. Each time Hudson made out with Stephen's ass, he swore he was being tortured. The ripening his body was undergoing was raw. He was raw. Ready for a pounding.

The sweat on his armpits thickened. The scent of anticipation was in the air. Hudson's oohs and gasps as he suckled Stephen's ass were an invitation to spread his legs even wider and lift his ass higher.

He pushed his butt at Hudson's tongue and wiggled his ass in a circular motion. Hudson followed Stephen's movement, sassily gliding his tongue in the same circular direction. Because his body was so alive, Stephen came close to smacking the chair. Each nerve was alert, prickles of lust ready to explode from the heat of Hudson's saliva and lapping tongue.

Not even when they were teenagers had it ever felt this good between them. The here and now was the best moment of Stephen's life, having the man he wanted above all others lavishing him with enticing laps and sassy kisses.

When Hudson's tongue didn't delve but plunged deep up inside Stephen's asshole, he thought he'd explode from the pleasure rippling through him. He cried out, still clinging to the chair. The tongue was exploring his insides, opening him to what his asshole truly wanted—Hudson's cock.

As if reading Stephen's mind, Hudson slowly withdrew his tongue. His lips were on Stephen's butt cheek, kissing his too-ripe skin. That was when from the corner of his eye he caught the lube and condom on the kitchen table.

Earlier, he'd heard a drawer open. Stephen tensed. All along Hudson had planned on fucking him in the kitchen. Everything had been formulated, right down to their conversation after dinner.

Part of Stephen shouted he'd been set up, that something nefarious awaited him after they were done fucking, but as much as his brain begged for him to get out while he stood a chance, he couldn't move. He let Hudson draw apart his ass cheeks. The sound of the foil being removed from the condom wrapper crackled in Stephen's ears. He held his breath, knowing Hudson would lube up his cock.

He couldn't get out and leave. Not now. Instead, he bent at the waist to give Hudson ample room to penetrate him.

Hudson didn't disappoint. The head of his cock was breaching Stephen. It'd been well over two years since he'd last had sex. But Hudson was good to him, as if somehow knowing, because his head remained inside Stephen and the rest of his erection was outside.

"You okay? Hmm?" Hudson's lips were warm on Stephen's ear.

Hearing those reassuring words, that Hudson cared enough about Stephen's comfort to ask, was water washing away the uncertainty tensing the back of his neck. He nodded.

"I'm gonna go slow. 'Kay? It's been a while for you?" Hudson's lips were back against Stephen's ear.

Stephen nodded. "A very long time."

"Hmm . . . as your nurse practitioner, I've analyzed everything, and you have a clean bill of health, but I think it's time you made an appointment at the station for a full checkup in my office, on my exam table . . ." There was a chuckle to Hudson's suggestion. He slipped his cock in a wee bit more. "You do know you'll have to strip down and wear a gown . . ."

"And what makes you think I already haven't?" Stephen couldn't believe their conversation, but it was so them to talk about this kind of stuff while having sex. "Maybe I already made an appointment for a . . . physical."

"I knew you were always a good boy. Next time I'm raw dogging you, baby." Hudson's words were wicked, the devil teasing.

Stephen was undergoing the stuffing of all stuffings. And it hurt, but the kind of hurt that made him bite his lower lip and welcome the discomfort, because there'd be tons of pleasure he'd receive once the pain subsided.

"I can hardly wait for you to fuck me," Hudson murmured. "This isn't *one time for old times*. There's gonna be lots of times. I'm a horny guy, y'know?"

Stephen's heart brightened. Yet their convo from earlier reminded him Hudson didn't want love anymore. Especially not Stephen's love. Still, he gritted out, "You think you're horny. Fuck me. I'm more than horny. I need your cock. Give it to me."

"You got it." Hudson gave Stephen's cheek a light slap and pumped.

The length and girth of Hudson's erection sliding up and into Stephen's ass was more than his hole could manage. He again bit down on his lower lip to take it all. His neck received kisses to soften the blow, and he reveled in the tender puckers on his nape.

The thrusts coming from Hudson grew quicker. His heavy breaths and groans were deep in Stephen's ear, his stocky body lying over his back. Hudson's strong hands fumbled for Stephen's half-hard dick.

Being touched from both ends was Stephen's undoing. His asshole was being stretched, forced to accommodate Hudson's lust demanding he open completely. Sighing, Stephen responded to his body's command to take it all.

Hudson's thrusts were long and deep, smooth rutting meant to taunt Stephen and stretch him. He didn't mind the pummeling. Earlier, Hudson had gifted Stephen with pure pleasure, and he was more than willing to reciprocate.

He held tight to the chair and let Hudson use him. Use him until Hudson's swift and fast fucking suddenly stopped, followed by low moans and husky gasps.

Stephen almost smiled, knowing he'd given Hudson what he wanted.

Chapter Ten: Hold on Loosely

Hudson chucked aside the pen. Concentration was impossible after last night's dinner and what had gone down in his kitchen. After they'd finished, Stephen had said he'd check his schedule to see when he could get Jesse to deejay for him again so they could *enjoy* another meal together.

Not knowing when he'd see Stephen hadn't stopped rolling through Hudson's mind all morning after he'd bid him goodnight.

Noon. Hudson had been trying to finish the paperwork for his last patient, who'd left ten minutes ago. If he poked his head out from his office, he'd probably find the RN and receptionist gone for lunch. He'd best get something to eat, too. His work cell phone rested on the desk — the phone he always scooped up and pocketed in case an emergency occurred and he had to hightail it back to work.

Once he locked up the place, he drove to Charlie's Chicken and Things to grab a bite. It was a smart of him to have ordered ahead. All he'd have to do was pull up a table and have his plate of food dropped in front of him.

The whisper had returned, poking the back of Hudson's head, telling him he was hoping to find Stephen at the one and only restaurant on the reserve. But Stephen had a half hour for lunch, and Hudson's heart shrank because he'd most likely be eating alone. For all he knew, Stephen could be on supervisory duty while the kids ate their meals at their desks before going outside to play since he taught grade six.

Then there was the two-spirit group meetings in Stephen's

classroom at four-thirty. If Hudson hightailed it after work, he could make the meeting.

See? You're looking for excuses to see him. Face it. Every plan you have produced so far has backfired, all because you love him.

Hudson thumped the steering wheel.

But he'd go to the meeting after work.

Hudson pulled up in the school's parking lot. With the weather cold enough to freeze his balls, he raced from his truck and dashed inside the school. As he headed for the meeting classroom, his big boots squeaked along the floor. At four thirty-five, the halls were empty of students and staff.

He was in the elementary portion that connected with the high school.

Talking carried into the hall, then laughter. Hudson followed the direction of the voices, passing lockers and posters on the wall, one reading *Be Red and Proud*, and another spelling out *P-R-I-D-E*.

He poked his head inside the classroom to find Stephen sitting on the desk. Seated in the student desks in the front row were two girls, one with a pixie type of haircut and the other with long flowing hair, a boy with the hood to his hoodie drawn up, and the one who identified as non-binary with big blue glasses and a mix of piercings in their nose, lip, and earlobes.

"Hello." Hudson offered a smile and shrugged off his parka.

"Students, I'm sure you know Mr. Suggashie. Say hello. Hudson, this is Tiffany, Melinda, Tyson, and Mackenzie."

"I know who they are. I see them around. I'm glad to be a part of your group." Hudson slipped his parka over the chair at one of the desks. He really had to get more involved the way Stephen was. Then again, being a teacher, even a deejay, gave Stephen an advantage over Hudson, who mainly dealt with diabetes patients, since the disease was rampant through the reserve.

"You've been *out* for a long time, Mr. Suggashie." The curious statement came from the boy named Tyson, who seemed to climb out of his hoodie. "Like, eons ago, wasn't that a scary time back then?"

Hudson almost laughed because the boy's statement made him to be around eighty years old. "Yeah, I've been out. I had a lot of help from my kokum."

"Really? She didn't mind?" This came from the girl named Tiffany who sported the short hair.

"No. She knew about the two-spirit people from the old days. She learned it from her kokum. Mr. Brandt probably told you the two-spirit were revered in the days of our ancestors, before the Europeans came over and frowned upon it, and taught us to frown upon it."

"Yeah, he gave us the history when the group first started." Mackenzie's cheeks colored. They ducked their head, and their silver hooped earrings rocked back and forth from the fast movement.

"My kokum did the same thing for me. She taught me not to be ashamed of who I am. She told me to be proud." Hudson peeked at Stephen, whose cheeks had also reddened.

"Mr. Brandt told us his father was against who he truly is." Melinda's voice was as soft-spoken as Stephen's, and she stared at her hands. "My dad was the same way at first. He didn't want me coming to these meetings, but my mom didn't mind. She . . . she was a big help. I guess my dad didn't care that I . . . well, I think girls are cool."

Melinda peeked at Tiffany.

Hudson rubbed his chin. Perhaps Melinda and Tiffany had been experiencing what he and Stephen had endured in high school. It was obvious the two pretty girls were sweet on each other. Maybe they were an item, but he couldn't outright ask them, although he could pose his inquiry to Stephen after the meeting was done.

"I brought some sage to burn while we meet. I hope this is okay." Hudson dug into his pocket.

"I . . . that's a great idea. I never thought about opening the meeting the way the elders do." Stephen cleared his throat.

"Before we do anything important, it's good to have the blessing of Creator." Hudson hoped he wasn't stepping on any toes. "If nobody minds."

"That sounds cool." Mackenzie glanced at Stephen.

"Is everyone in favor?" Stephen asked. "It is our tradition."

"Sure." Given the glow of Tiffany's dark eyes, she was eager to have the sage burned.

The meetings only lasted an hour so the kids could be home in time for supper, Stephen had mentioned. When they finished, Hudson had been treated to each student's story. Mackenzie had been teased mercilessly at first but was now comfortable identifying as non-binary. Melinda had it tougher because her father still silently brooded about her orientation but was no longer vocal about his opinion. As for Tiffany, who was raised in a single-parent household, her mother was proud of her daughter and stood by her. Tyson lived with his uncle, aunt, and cousins, and the family supported him.

The students left the room with a *Seeya on Friday*, leaving Hudson and Stephen alone.

Stephen got off the desktop where he'd sat for the meeting. He began wiping down the whiteboard.

Hudson should leave, too. But his feet were rooted to the floor, refusing to allow him to vacate the classroom. "Tiffany and Melinda . . . they . . . do they give you déjà vu?" Great, even his mouth had a mind of its own. No part on his body was listening to his brain.

Stephen's shoulders tightened. "Yeah." His voice was smaller than a whisper.

Hudson glanced at his parka and back to Stephen, who continued to clean the whiteboard as if trying to strip it of any imperfections. "Everything okay?"

"Yeah."

The tips of Hudson's fingers tingled. He was on the verge of marching up to Stephen, removing the cloth from his hand, and tossing the damned thing in the garbage. "Did you ask Jesse about filling in, then?"

This time Stephen stopped wiping the board and pivoted. His knitted brows relaxed. "I haven't had time to ask him yet. But I'll call him tonight."

A twitch erupted at the back of Hudson's neck. He couldn't start doubting, but Stephen not calling right away meant . . . what? He cleared his throat. "Too bad you can't run the channel all day and night."

"I told you already it'd be a lot of work." Stephen moved to the desk and plunked his sexy ass back on top. He crossed his black dress shoes at the ankles. "Like I said, I'd have to quit my job, and I can't do that. Not with Mom's medical condition. And we're going into the 'Peg on Wednesday."

"Wednesday?" Hudson had to stop himself from sputtering. "What for?"

"To see the specialist. She always sees him on a regular basis." Stephen picked at the cloth he still held.

Well, yeah, Hudson knew that, because he set up her appointments with the rheumatologist, but it wasn't like he memorized every patient's file on their whereabouts with other doctors they'd see.

"Just overnight. We'll be back for Thursday. I have someone subbing for me. Jesse's handling the show for Wednesday night, so I'm kind of leery about asking him again."

Hudson relaxed with the answer he'd gotten and why Stephen hadn't been keen on calling Jesse right away. "I get it. Your station, your responsibility, hey?"

"He loves broadcasting. If he had his way, he'd do it all the time, but he has a job, too."

Hudson understood. Jesse was an unfortunate high school dropout and worked at the gas bar. "Do you think he'll ever take radio broadcasting? Go back to school?"

"I'm working on him." Stephen flashed his perfectly straight white teeth. "I'm a teacher. Of course I want everyone to have an education."

"So . . . you're going overnight?"

Stephen nodded.

Well, they were only supposed to be fuck buddies, at Hudson's stupid insistence, and fuck buddies didn't tell each other intimate details, like taking their mom into the city. Oh geez. The city. What if Stephen went to a gay bar and found a hookup since he wasn't getting *any* this week? He had every right to. They weren't a couple. They didn't owe each other anything.

Hudson stumbled away from the desk and dragged his feet across the floor until he stood where Stephen sat.

Stephen tilted his head, peering curiously.

Hudson placed his hands on each side of Stephen's outer thighs and wormed his way between his slightly open legs. A shot of breath dusted Hudson's face from Stephen's gasp. Being in such a snug spot was pure heat to Hudson's crotch. He slid his mouth over Stephen's to taste warm lips easily melting against his own.

He wasn't after a hot kiss, more like something tender, so Stephen would remember who was waiting for him when he returned.

Even though they'd seen each other yesterday, a lifetime had passed. Hudson's heart had forgotten how much he'd ached for this man's presence when they'd been teenagers, but his head reminded him he was supposed to make Stephen pay for all the pain he'd caused. If only Hudson's damned heart would get with the fucking program. Even his tongue couldn't resist and slipped between Stephen's soft lips.

When Stephen gently explored Hudson's mouth, the ache in his heart vanished. Neither did he expect to have Stephen slide off the desk and wrap his arms Hudson's shoulders, drawing them together as one.

He stood there, melted against Stephen, savoring the lazy exploration of their tongues. Whereas at first he'd wanted to steal a simple kiss, his growing cock had other plans. And Hudson's excitement only intensified because Stephen's erection was pressing on Hudson's belly.

He broke the kiss, his breaths coming quickly. "I want you," he murmured.

The fire in Stephen's eyes mirrored the same feeling Hudson was undergoing. "I want you, too."

"We got time before you're due at the radio station."

"I go on at six."

"There's always time for a quickie." Hudson licked Stephen's earlobe and caressed his thigh. "If you wanna be on time, we can do it at the station."

"The station." Stephen clung to Hudson. "Let's go. Do you got anything?"

"Always." Hudson forced himself to break from their embrace. "I'll meet you there."

"Okay. Give me five to lock up."

Hudson turned and strode to the desk. He grabbed his parka. Here he was, supposed to hold on loosely, just like the .38 Special song said to do when it came to another person, but his fear was a monster ready to swallow him whole, because he couldn't seem to leave Stephen alone.

CHAPTER ELEVEN: JUST CAN'T LEAVE YOU ALONE

Hudson raced his truck to Main where the old radio station was located. He reached inside the glove compartment, the spot he'd stashed the extra bottle of lube he'd purchased at the pharmacy in Red Lake. How pathetic. What kind of moron went driving around with lube on hand and condoms in his console?

Someone desperate, that was who.

He turned the wheel and guided the vehicle into the plowed parking lot. Not that it was a true parking lot. Simply a spot cleared to accommodate two cars. The wooden building would be locked, so he'd have to wait for Stephen to arrive.

The lube was cold in Hudson's hand, frozen since it was water based. His thighs were the perfect place to warm up the stuff. Hopefully he could thaw the bottle before they got busy, or they were up shit creek with no paddle for the canoe.

People loved Stephen's show, and they'd voiced their hope for having a full-time station again, like Russel had done for them, offering news reports, updates around the reserve, and music. Russel had even hosted election debates, besides interviewing people in the community. It'd been a fun station.

Winnipeg. Hudson drummed his fingers on the steering wheel. Maybe they could get away one weekend if Jesse was willing to man the channel. But there was Mrs. Brandt to consider. Did she still favor her husband's side when it came to

Stephen? Should he ask? No, he didn't have a right to, not after suggesting they only be friends with benefits.

Stephen's SUV appeared. The black vehicle pulled in beside Hudson's truck.

They got out at the same time to the frigid cold that continued to haunt the reserve.

"Let's hurry." Stephen held his key set in his gloved hand.

Hudson's teeth chattered. "I'm glad they supply hydro to this place. Your equipment would freeze."

"Me, too." Stephen darted up the shoveled path and ran up the four stairs.

Hudson was right behind him, almost melting into Stephen for any kind of body warmth.

After a few tries and some rattling, much to Hudson's impatience, Stephen got the door open. "They need to refit this thing."

"They do. Did you tell maintenance?" Hudson asked. "A guy could lose his balls out here trying to unlock the stupid thing."

They dashed inside. Both stamped their boots on the mat to a cozy room with the computer and audio equipment set up in front of a glass window facing another room where Russell had previously hosted his interviews. On hand was a leather chair, pushed into the deejay's station. A mini fridge was in the corner, and another chair.

Stephen hung his coat on the tree rack, teeth chattering. He held out his hand. Hudson removed his hand from his jacket pocket. In the process, the bottle of lube fell out and hit the wooden floor with a loud clunk.

"Uh . . ." Stephen winced. "Frozen?"

"Yeah." Hudson shrugged sheepishly. "But there're other things we can do. Why don't you park your ass in the chair?"

"Uh-uh." Stephen wagged his finger. "I've yet to suck yours. You get in the chair."

"Gladly." Hudson sank in the plush leather and unzipped his pants. His slight roll was on full view under the light above them, and he grimaced.

Stephen chuckled.

His soft laugh reassured Hudson he was perfect the way he was. "I gotta hit the gym, too. I've been walking everywhere."

"Gym. Walking." Stephen bore down on him. "It doesn't matter." He settled between Hudson's open legs. "Too bad I couldn't have done this to you in my classroom."

"Kinky." Hudson snickered.

"But I can't afford to get fired. And seeing my desk in the morning when the students arrive . . . yeah, not quite want I want to envision while teaching." Stephen slid his palms over Hudson's thighs. His gaze was trained not on Hudson's dick, but his eyes . . . There was warmth in Stephen's gaze, the kind a lover would cast to their significant other, not a fuck friend.

"Yeah?" Hudson stroked Stephen's cheekbone. "Don't wanna be thinking about blowing a guy while lecturing the class, hey?"

"Hardly." Stephen leaned in and glided his mouth over Hudson's.

The kiss matched the warmth Hudson had spied earlier in Stephen's eyes—tender and full of . . . he stiffened. Stephen must not have noticed the tension, because he kept exploring Hudson's mouth in that soft, dreamy fashion. Damn, the kisses were as gentle and lulling as Stephen.

Hudson couldn't resist easing his hands up inside Stephen's sweater. Instead of meeting skin, his palms brushed linen. He'd forgotten about the shirt. One thing about winter—too many layers of clothes. With how frigid the weather was, Stephen probably had an undershirt beneath his collared shirt, too. Well, he couldn't blame the guy. Hudson had his own layers to work through, like long underwear beneath his jeans.

"Hmm . . . too many clothes," Stephen murmured.

"You read my mind. I was thinking the same thing." His lips continued to brush Stephen's. "I was also thinking about my long underwear."

"Yeah?" Stephen arched his brow. "Let's see. Rubber duckies? Teddy bears?"

The chuckle raced from Hudson's mouth. "Hate to disappoint you. Plain ol' boring gray. What about you?"

"Same thing. Boring gray."

"I guess we gotta live it up, hey?" Hudson worked the linen shirt loose from the waist of Stephen's pants.

"Shouldn't I be the one taking your shirt out?" Stephen's suggestion was hot on Hudson's mouth, and those blue eyes were so intense they almost penetrated his black ones.

"You can take care of my pants. Never mind the shirt. I got the same shit going on that you do. Sweater, shirt, and undershirt." Heart pounding, Hudson traced his finger along Stephen's cheekbone.

Stephen squatted between Hudson's thighs. When his long fingers wrapped Hudson's button to his jeans, his muscles constricted with anticipation. The button gave, and his zipper lowered. He lifted his butt slightly off the comfortable leather chair. As his jeans and long underwear were worked around his hips to give Stephen access to his hard cock, Hudson groaned.

Stephen didn't suck right away. He gently gripped Hudson's length, staring at his dick. Hudson tried to peer at Stephen's eyes, but all he could catch was the top of his black hair.

"Oh, man, you got such a nice cock." The breath from Stephen's mouth skimmed the tip of Hudson's prick.

Before Hudson could reply, the head of his erection received a delicate kiss that flooded the tips of his fingers and toes with heat. He gasped. Stephen's mouth encircled the tip, engulfing Hudson in a bed of warm flesh and saliva. He groaned, settling in the chair. His fingers automatically reached for Stephen's hair, and he stroked the silky locks.

It'd been a long time since he'd last gotten some suction. Stephen's mouth hadn't disappointed in their youth and sure didn't disappoint in the present. Hudson kept stroking the black strands while his erection received a luscious long lick from the base all the way to the tip.

The attention Stephen was showering on Hudson's cock was more than two guys banging boots. Not only was he getting sucked off, but silky caresses were also bestowed on his balls, and his prick continued to be licked from top to bottom. Even the head of his dick received a tender kiss. The sensual worshiping was something a lover would do.

Hudson gulped.

He's making love to my cock.

He squeezed his eyes tight. Aw fuck, his heart was speaking again, telling him this was what he secretly wanted. But love meant a knife in the back. And Stephen couldn't be trusted. Yet the stupid little voice kept nagging, insisting Stephen was honorable, and his father was the jerk who'd ruined what they'd had going in their youth. Being so young, of course Stephen hadn't possessed the fortitude to stand up to the man he called dad.

Hudson shooed away the insane thoughts. He'd enjoy his blow job. Nothing more.

When Stephen slowly took Hudson's dick between his lips, Hudson gritted his teeth. The suction was incredible, and for a moment his heart seemed to stop beating. Not only was his body being teased into submission, but his brain was about to pop from Stephen's mouth imprisoning Hudson's length. The continuous gliding up and down from the tip to the base was enough to drive him insane.

Stephen's head bobbed. The smacking and sucking noises

coming from him were pure pleasure to Hudson's ears. His ex-boyfriend sounded as if he was enjoying every minute of tasting hard cock.

The pressure of Stephen's lips working their magic was coaxing Hudson's sack full of jizz to release itself. Already, the pleasure was building in his balls and rushing to the slit in the top of his dick. The crackling euphoria was forming, close to exploding from within, and he held tighter to Stephen's hair while thrusting faster.

Fucking Stephen's mouth was as hot as fucking his ass. The electric excitement was rippling through Hudson. He stiffened and released his jizz straight into Stephen's waiting mouth.

Hudson continued to groan, his butt half off the chair as he held tight to Stephen's head. The small ripples of electricity still quaked through Hudson's limbs, and he didn't want the euphoria to end.

"Oh, man . . ." He couldn't stop gasping and searching for a breath. He swiped at his forehead. "Damn . . ." He opened his eyes to Stephen's sensual grin, and a smidgen of cum lingered at the corner of his mouth.

"You missed a spot." Hudson drew his finger along the sticky wetness.

Stephen sucked Hudson's finger between his lips.

Hudson shivered. Hell, he'd just come, and he was about ready to blow another load. "You're stopping by after your show's done. It's my turn to get some up the ass."

"Yeah?" Stephen's lips hovered around Hudson's slowly softening cock. "I'd love to, but I promised Mom I'd get her some chicken after I leave here." Disappointment threaded through his reply.

Hudson's stomach sank. "Can't you drop off the chicken and then stop back here?" Friends with benefits weren't supposed to say that. They weren't even supposed to be friends.

Merely fuck buddies.

Stephen's gaze drifted to the console.

"That's quite the boner you got. I wanna take care of it." Hudson used his lips to point at Stephen's bulging crotch.

"Yeah, I sure do." Stephen's gaze drifted back to Hudson. "Okay. I'll stop by after I drop off Mom's chicken."

"I know it'll be late. and we both got work in the morning . . ." Hudson calculated the traveling.

Stephen would have to pick up the chicken, drive up to the Seven Mile, and then make the drive back to Main. Once they were finished with their booty call, Stephen would have to make another drive up to the Seven Mile.

Stephen finally nodded. "It's okay. I'll be there."

"I'll see you after your show, and I'll make sure and tune in." Hudson couldn't resist another kiss.

Stephen slipped from the SUV to the icy cold attempting to find its way into his clothing. His face stung from the shivering air daring to try and freeze his exposed skin. Everyone would call him crazy if they knew he was going to this extreme for sex. But it was more than sex. Being asked back to Hudson's house meant his former lover was thawing.

The Hudson that Stephen had known in the past would've never made such a suggestion, not the vindictive man whose scorn knew no mercy. If he was patient, Stephen stood a chance.

He scooted up the walkway he always kept shoveled and salted so Mom wouldn't unnecessarily slip. Walking was hard for her, no thanks to the disease attacking the joints on the soles of her feet that had created bulging thick balls. Grandma had also suffered from rheumatoid arthritis, and so had Great-Grandma.

Stephen shivered because the autoimmune disease was

inheritable. All he could hope for was once he reached his late forties, it wouldn't attack him, too. But he was Mom's only child. She had to pass the disease to someone, and he was the only someone.

He threw open the back door, and the cold followed him inside. The utility door was closed, containing the frigid air within the room. Since Mom hated messes, he made sure to slip off his big boots that kept his toes warm and cozy.

"Stephen?" Mom called out.

"I got your chicken." He kept his parka on and entered the kitchen and adjoining living room. "Did you want me to get you a plate?"

"Please." Mom had the Aboriginal Peoples Television Network on, her favorite channel. She was watching the news.

Stephen strode over to the cupboard and retrieved a plate. He also grabbed some cutlery and ketchup.

Mom's lubricating drops sat on the end table — the disease also attacked her eyes and made them extremely dry. Already she'd had her corneas replaced because the woodstove heat had been too hot for her to handle and had created ulcers on them. So Stephen had installed propane to run an electric furnace, which was less drying for Mom and easier on her eyes. Of course, purchasing the fuel was super-expensive, but they had no choice.

The humidifier ran on the end table, letting out steamy moisture to keep Mom's eyes hydrated.

Stephen fixed up the dinner tray in front of Mom's spot and set her chicken on top, along with the plate, cutlery, and condiments. "Did you want anything to drink?" Evenings were difficult for her, a time when her joints were at their worst. The temperature didn't help either.

"Please." Her voice was soft.

He glanced at her finger braces in their usual spot instead of on her fingers to keep her joints from becoming disfigured.

Grandma's fingers had shifted to the side, making it difficult for her to do anything, and if Mom didn't start following her therapy, she'd face the same fate.

Stephen opened the fridge and grabbed the pitcher of filtered water, Mom's go-to drink. He poured a glass while glancing her way.

How could he leave her again? His guilt was already great from working all day and deejaying in the evening. His free time, even his half hour lunch break, was spent checking on her so she wouldn't become lonely now that Dad was gone. At least her friends stopped in during the day to keep her company. She couldn't craft because of the pain she experienced in the small joints of her hands. But she had plenty of audio books on hand.

Stephen stared at the phone. He had to call Hudson and tell him he couldn't come. Somehow, he had to make Hudson understand Stephen's true purpose for moving home was to care for Mom. But Hudson hadn't shown any understanding in the past, so Stephen would probably get an earful, maybe even a *fuck off*.

Chapter Twelve: Take Me through the Night

Now that Mom was settled in to watch the news and eat her chicken, Stephen slipped into his bedroom to make the call he dreaded dialing. He should've bought himself something to eat, too, because his stomach growled from missing dinner and only scarfing down a light lunch because of recess duty.

He stared at his cell phone and forced himself to press the button for Hudson's number while pacing back and forth in his small bedroom that could only hold his bed and a tiny chest of drawers. Whenever he needed to work, he used the spare room where he had his desk set up.

Hudson picked up on the first ring. "What's up?" Tension crackled in his tone.

Stephen fisted and unfisted his hand. "I got bad news. Mom's not feeling too well." He shouldn't lie. The truth was better.

"Oh? What's wrong?" The tension vanished, and concern was in Hudson's voice. "Is there anything I can do?"

There was no surprise Hudson was concerned. He was Mom's nurse practitioner and helped her manage the disease. "No. We'll talk to her specialist about it. He'll most likely send you the report when we meet with him on Wednesday afternoon."

"She has a 'script for codeine if she is in severe pain. Did she take one?"

"Not that I know of." Stephen sat on the edge of the single bed. He'd best spit out the truth. "Honestly, she's about the same . . . I . . . I just feel . . . she's alone all day," he sputtered and threw out his hand. "I can't leave her again. I can't. You know how hard this disease has been on her. I feel . . . even my show . . . I was already in Red Lake for the weekend. I can't keep . . . I moved back to help her."

"I see . . ."

The silence was strong enough to pop Stephen's eardrums. Ever since they'd started speaking again, he'd been bending over backward to accommodate Hudson, but Stephen couldn't let past guilts keep dictating his decisions. "I'm sorry about this."

"Then I guess we'll get together when you get back from Winnipeg." There wasn't any trace of annoyance or disturbance in Hudson's reply.

Great, now this reintroduced Stephen's guilt. "I'm really sorry."

"Call me when you can get Jesse to fill in. Bye."

The line went dead. Stephen almost threw the phone against the wall. As a substitute, he let the cell drop to the homemade quilt on his bed Mom had made before her rheumatoid arthritis had gone into full attack mode.

They couldn't get on the same page. At this point, he wasn't sure what Hudson wanted. If it was only sex, why should he become angry, annoyed, or disappointed?

He doesn't trust me, that's why. And he has every right not to trust me after I refused to accept his love. So why would he hand it over a second time?

Maybe finding a peace offering in the city might help? No, it'd take more than a peace offering. If trust was broken, it had to be restored, and Stephen would have to restore the trust by coming clean with what he wanted and earn Hudson's love again.

He'd start by taking Hudson out for dinner once he came

back from the city and find out if he'd be a winner or a second-time loser at love.

Hudson stared at his second helping of beef stew mixed with carrots, onions, and potatoes. Another evening spent alone after getting the brush-off from Stephen the night before. He ran his spoon through the chunky bits of vegetables and meat. After work, he'd made a loaf of bannock and had already polished off three slices while contemplating a fourth. No, he wouldn't. He'd stick to his diet and finish what he had in his bowl. No more drowning his sorrow in food.

Earlier, he'd turned on his laptop and brought up the website to Stephen's radio show, which played another song. What a way to spend the night. Yes, he could understand Mrs. Brandt came first. He had no problem if Stephen wanted to spend time with his mother. Maybe what pinched Hudson's heart was too many lonely nights sitting by himself after work. And he had nobody to blame but himself.

He had signed up at the fire department as a volunteer. His first training session started next week. On Saturday morning, he had plans to snowshoe with two buddies. But a man in his thirties didn't desire to sit by himself. He wanted to come home to someone, talk about his day, spend the night watching TV or a movie, cuddle by the woodstove and enjoy the fire.

His cell phone lay silent on top of the table. He reached over and typed in a message.

I have a request. I'd like to hear Take Me Through the Night.

Maybe Stephen would find the underlying meaning within the lyrics. The song was about a lonely man who'd ended a relationship with much regret, and was still full of regret, wishing for the love he'd lost to get him through the night.

His finger hovered above the *send* button. He grimaced and hit *send*.

Nothing appeared in response to his text. He reached for his spoon and slid the stew into his mouth. After eating a few spoonfuls, he glanced at his phone, but nothing still showed on the screen. He shoveled more stew between his teeth. The screen continued to remain blank.

Pathetic. He came close to knocking his forehead against the table in disgust.

To make matters worse, the screen on his phone went black.

Just as he spooned up another helping of stew, his phone dinged.

He tossed aside his spoon and greedily reached for his cell. If the black piece of equipment was food, he would've wolfed it down in one bite. He slid the locked screen open to the message.

Not a problem. You do know friends always take one another through a rough night, don't you?

Hudson almost choked on the piece of carrot he continued to chew. He quickly typed in . . .

Yeah, they do. But my friends are home with their wives or girlfriends. What about you?

He wiped his mouth and reached for his milk to wash away the last of the broth.

Going home to Mom once I finish here. I meant to text you after I was done.

Hudson hiccupped.

Yeah? What about?

He drummed his fingers on the table, but no response came. Maybe Stephen was doing something for the show which was why he'd gone silent.

Hudson rose and set his bowl and plate in the sink full of soapy water. While he washed the dishes, he kept sneaking peeks at his phone. The darn thing finally dinged.

He wiped off his hands and scooped up the cell.

About why you're asking me to play Take Me Through the Night.

His mouth went dry. *What do you mean?*

I was thinking last night, and we need to talk.

Hudson's heartbeat kicked into overdrive. *Talk about what?*

How about dinner on Saturday night? That's when Mom goes to the senior center to play bingo.

Okay. I'll cook. Is Jesse filling in?

Yes.

Then have a good trip tomorrow. Don't do anything I wouldn't do.

I'm not doing anything. Once we see the specialist, I'm taking Mom shopping, out for dinner, and then back to the hotel.

Any fears Hudson had about Stephen sneaking off to a gay bar to get laid vanished.

Then I'll see you Saturday night.

Stephen stood in a gift shop at the St. Vital Mall, one of the many neighborhoods in Winnipeg. Mom's appointment had gone about the same as last time. If only she'd cast aside her fear and had seen a doctor right away instead of denying she'd had rheumatoid arthritis, the treatment that was offered could've helped and slowed the damage to her joints. But she'd waited until Dad had insisted.

If Stephen ever experienced symptoms, he was consulting a doctor right away. The magic number in his family was forty-eight, according to Mom. That was when the autoimmune disease showed its ugly head. He had a long way to go before he reached two years before his golden birthday, but he wouldn't let fear stop him, as it had stopped Mom. Now she was in the worst position possible at fifty-nine.

Too bad Dad was no longer with them. He'd been great taking care of Mom and ensuring she followed her therapy to the letter, something Stephen had told her she must continue if he was moving back to help her.

At least they'd avoided talking about Hudson on the plane. Dad's disapproval had directly influenced Mom's feelings about Stephen's former lover.

Now he'd have to arrange to have one of the ladies at the senior center drive Mom home after bingo.

"Did you find what you were looking for?"

Stephen jumped and turned as Mom approached, using her cane. Red stained her cheeks. He knew she was embarrassed about having to use one for long walks at her age, but hiking through the mall was too hard for her to do without assistance.

"Oh, cologne?" Mom glanced over the different bottles and colors on the display shelf. "Are you getting a new one?"

Maybe Stephen should reconsider on the cologne. Knowing Hudson, he'd probably think he stank if he received such a gift. "No . . . uh . . . well . . ."

"Can I help you?" The clerk scooted up to them with teeth whiter than a toothpaste commercial, a tan bronzer than a statue, and hair tousled on top and buzzed at the sides. His scent, a crisp aqua aroma, reached them before he did. "Are you seeking something new or deciding to finally take the plunge and . . . Wait." He held up his hand. "After Evening, by Cleo LaSalle." He leaned in and sniffed.

Stephen's cheeks heated. "Uh . . . yes."

"I know my designers, hon." The clerk winked. "Now, what would you like to try?"

Stephen might as well go through with the gift. He had to bring Hudson something to know he'd been on Stephen's mind while in Winnipeg, especially if he wanted their conversation and his second chance to go over with favor and not hit a brick wall. "I, well, I need something that's, err . . . not very powerful."

"Discreet?" The clerk arched a smooth brow.

"Yeah, that's the perfect word." Stephen nodded.

Mom moved in closer. She peered at the glass counter.

"Give me one sec. I have something that I know you'll love." The clerk rummaged around beneath the counter while staring up at Stephen, grinning. His green eyes twinkled. "Mind you, the scent you're wearing is hardly discreet. After Evening is about a good time spent between the sheets, or a man out to attract someone for his sheets."

More heat climbed onto Stephen's cheeks. This was so personal, however, to buy a gift, he needed the clerk to invade his privacy, but as for Mom hovering behind him, and people walking up and down the main aisle in the department store, glancing his way, he could do without them. "It's for a . . . friend."

"A friend?" The clerk grabbed the tester. He laid his hand on the counter. "He must be pretty special. This is a man's cologne."

"Oh, I know." Stephen cleared his throat. Why couldn't the clerk speak quieter? He might as well shout since Mom was right there.

"Tell me about him." The clerk grabbed a couple of more testers. "Is he an outdoors man? Snowmobiler? Hunter?"

"He's a nurse practitioner. He . . . uh . . . he enjoys the outdoors. He's not the kind of man to wear cologne, but he might for . . . special occasions." Stephen couldn't stop his stammering.

Mom moved in closer.

Stephen could feel her eyes drilling into him.

The clerk spritzed the first bottle. "This is an idea of the scent, but keep in mind scent changes depending on the person. What do you think?"

A clean, airy aroma wafted under Stephen's nostrils. The clerk sure knew his stuff. The cologne was every inch Hudson. "That's it. He'd like that."

"Lucky man." The clerk glanced down to the bottles. "What size would you like . . . if you're a size queen." He cackled at his own joke.

More heat spread across Stephen's face. Gosh, who knew buying cologne could be so embarrassing. "Let's start with the . . . err . . . smallest first. If he likes it, I can always get him the bigger bottle."

Mom's eyeballs were pretty much pushing into his shoulders now. He craned his neck.

She held his stare. "He put you through a lot of heartache," she murmured as the clerk boxed up the cologne.

"But he's a nice man, and it's apparent he's interested in you." She moved in beside him and shoved her chin at the metrosexual clerk.

A hint of shock bumped up Stephen's spine. Dad hadn't been too keen on Stephen dating men when he'd been away at university or while teaching in southern Ontario, but Mom seemed to have done a one-eighty. Maybe she hadn't minded him being gay? Maybe what she minded was . . . Hudson?

Stephen opened his wallet and removed his bank card. "What do you mean?"

"It took you a year to make up your mind to go away to university or not." She kept speaking quietly. "You don't know how worried I was about you."

"I went the next year." Stephen handed over his bank card.

The clerk began wrapping the cologne in blue paper.

"A man that demanding will always be demanding. I should know. I was married to such a man." Mom kept staring. "Don't get me wrong. I loved your father very much."

"You think Hudson's demanding?" Stephen punched in his PIN.

"Considering you weren't ready to come out and he didn't show you any respect, but upped and left, yes, I'd say that's demanding." She laid her palm on his forearm. "I just don't want to see you hurt again."

She was right. While Hudson had bolted for Winnipeg and shacked up with this Leonard guy he'd mentioned, Stephen had remained at the reserve in a black hole, spending the summer and into the fall going through the motions at the radio station, and then hiding away under his covers at night to cry away the heartache over losing the only man he'd knew he'd ever love.

What if he ended up in the same mess again? Hudson did say he wasn't permanently remaining at the reserve. His contract was for two years.

CHAPTER THIRTEEN: TAKE ME BACK

The drive to the community center was silent. Mom stared out the passenger window at blackness while Stephen kept his eye on the snow-covered, icy, gravel road.

"Did you bring your dabbers?" That was a dumb question, and Stephen cringed. Of course Mom had brought her bingo paraphernalia.

She nodded.

"Mom . . ."

"You're a grown man." She kept her voice quiet and continued to stare out the window. "I can't tell you not to see him."

At least she understood and gave him the proper room an adult child required. He'd packed an overnight bag, just in case. He'd keep it in the vehicle if he found himself going home with his tail tucked between his legs.

"You're nervous."

"Uh . . . nervous?" He glanced at her.

"You're rubbing the steering wheel. You always rub something when you're nervous."

"Yeah, I can admit I'm nervous." He entered the main part of the reserve. The twinkling stars above vanished from the amount of light being cast from the homes and buildings. The gift he'd bought in Winnipeg sat on the console.

He pulled up to the main entrance at the community center.

Mom laid her hand over his. "Stay put. You don't always have to be catering to me. And remember what I told you. You deserve a good man. If Hudson can't see all the wonderful things about you, well . . ." She opened the door, grabbed her bingo bag, and got out.

"G'night, Mom."

"Goodnight."

He waited for her to make her way inside. Someone held open the door for her, and his chest warmed, but at the same time his heart sank. Why did the disease have to be so intense in his family?

He drove off, running his palms along the steering wheel. There was no rehearsed speech he'd prepared because what he had to say came from his heart. All he could hope for was that Hudson would give him a second chance. A real second chance.

To ensure the dinner was perfect, Hudson used the hand-held mixer to whip the potatoes instead of mashing them. He'd cooked a roast and had steamed a mixture of winter vegetables consisting of brussels sprouts, broccoli, cauliflower, and carrots. The table was set. He'd even lit candles. A fire crackled in the woodstove.

The ambience was perfect. He even had the radio show playing so they could enjoy the music Stephen had programmed for tonight's playlist. For the last two evenings, Hudson had even tuned in to Stephen's show while relaxing and doing paperwork he'd taken home from the nursing station.

Headlights appeared in the living room window — he'd yet to draw the curtains.

If Hudson were to take his blood pressure, he'd probably be one hundred and eighty over one hundred and twenty, having to write himself a prescription for a good beta-blocker and diuretic if he didn't settle down.

He shut off the mixer. A glop of potato caked his finger, which he licked off.

Okay, everything was perfect. Gravy simmering. Roast out of the oven and settling. Potatoes were officially done. The vegetables sat in a bowl warming on the oven.

The expected knock came at the door.

Hudson took a big breath and beelined for the utility room. He opened the door. In Stephen's hand was a wrapped blue package with a white bow on top.

Every nerve in Hudson's body jumped to life. "C'mon in."

For once, Stephen's scent, his sexy bod covered in a parka, and his devastating blue eyes, didn't bowl Hudson over. He couldn't stop staring at the present.

There wasn't much room for him to step back, which left Stephen no choice but to brush up against Hudson, who almost melted himself into the wall. Even after they'd had sex, and not once but twice, he was behaving like a crazy teenager about to pop his cherry.

"Err . . ." Hudson coughed. "I'll . . ." He finally managed to worm to the entryway leading to the kitchen. "Let me take your clothes." *Fuck!* "I mean lemme take your parka."

Stephen's grin was as delicious as his sensual scent. "Which is it? My clothes or my parka?"

Both. "You know what I mean." Hudson forced a chuckle.

"Considering what we did at the radio station, I was thinking you meant my clothes." Stephen unzipped the parka. He slipped off the heavy garment like a stripper at a bar Hudson had frequented in Winnipeg after getting dumped by lover number three to try and shake the disappointment suffocating him.

"You got anymore moves like that?" Now that Hudson had found a nip of courage, the joke easily rolled off his tongue.

"Like what?" Stephen set the parka on the washer next to

the door.

"Those stripper moves." Hudson held up his hands halfway and waggled his fingers. "I tossed plenty of loonies on-stage. I'm a pro."

Stephen's smile was as suggestive as the removal of his parka. "Oh? You did? I think I might have to fix that if you tend to sneak off and ogle strippers."

"Fix it? How?" Hudson shuffled backward into the kitchen.

"Maybe give you a private show?" Stephen ambled forward, pretty much bearing down on Hudson while holding the gift. "I got you something while I was in the city."

"Thanks." Hudson took the present. Part of him was disappointed Stephen abruptly kiboshed their flirting, because he sure wouldn't mind sampling a lap dance, but the other part couldn't wait to open what was inside the package. As he attempted to tear the paper, his hands shook.

Once Hudson had the gift open, all thoughts of a lap dance vanished. No, he hadn't expected anything extravagant, but the gesture of cologne, an outdoorsy, clean aroma at that, was perfect. Thought had gone into the purchase, because Stephen knew Hudson wasn't one for strong fragrances. At work, because of policy, he never wore anything scented. "Thank you."

"You're welcome." Stephen continued to stand at the entranceway of the utility room since Hudson was blocking him access to the kitchen.

"Err . . . C'mon in. Dinner's ready." Hudson motioned at the table. The dim lighting and candles screamed romance. Maybe he'd gone a bit over the top?

"Very nice." Stephen glanced around. His gaze centered on the crackling fire in the woodstove. "You're even playing the station."

"I wanted to hear your playlist for tonight, even if Jesse is deejaying." Hudson scampered to the kitchen counter. "I made a roast."

"Roast sounds great."

"Pork roast. I thought it'd be something different than beef again." Hudson picked up the knife he'd sharpened and the big fork.

"Anything you cook always tastes good." Stephen's voice seemed to be on the nape of Hudson's neck.

Hudson shivered. He stole a quick peek over his shoulder to find Stephen seated. The man had a way with skimming his words across Hudson's flesh, no matter how far away Stephen was, such as the night he'd heard him on the radio playing *Back Where You Belong*.

Tonight, Jesse had a run of glam rock from the seventies going on.

"Did you program this personally for . . . our dinner?" Hudson picked up the plate of pork roast and set it on the table.

"You have to admit, we were always on the same page when it came to music." Stephen took the whipped potatoes Hudson handed over.

"True. We did." Hudson plopped the bowl of steamed veggies down. He sat adjacent from Stephen instead of across from him. Bold move? Maybe. But Stephen did say he wanted to talk. "Help yourself."

They served up their dinners.

Hudson buttered a slice of bannock. "How'd your mom's appointment go?"

"The same as last time." With smooth slices, Stephen cut into his roast.

"I noticed you did that last time with your steak." Hudson used his fork to point. "I thought you'd stop that when you got out of your teens, but you still do it."

"What's that?" Stephen bit into his pork.

"Cut your meat before you eat, instead of cutting and eating." Hudson couldn't help his grin.

"Old habits die hard. You know it comes from Mom cutting up everything I ate when I was a little kid." Stephen chuckled. "It's a habit I can't shake."

"Everyone's moms did that. Well, except for mine." Hudson shrugged.

Stephen winced.

Hudson stiffened. "Don't feel bad. I'm not the first kid on the rez to be raised by his kokum, and I won't be the last."

"I know. Have you ever heard from her?" Stephen chewed.

"Course not." Why would Hudson hear from an alcoholic who chose booze over her own child? As far as he was concerned, Kokum was his mother, and Stephen was more than aware of that.

"I . . ." Stephen wiped his mouth. "I wanted to wait until after dinner, but I wouldn't mind talking now. I mean, tradition says to eat first . . ."

"It's okay. Talk away." Hudson tried to casually slide a spoonful of whipped potatoes into his mouth and swallow, but for once, instead of rolling down his throat, the creamy mess sat on his tongue.

"I . . ." Stephen shoved his fork around on his plate. "I . . . the dinner is really great. It is. Thanks for cooking."

Hudson could only nod since he'd yet to swallow the potatoes.

"I know we agreed to engage in only sex . . ." Stephen's gaze bobbed about. "I respect that. Y'know? But . . ." He drew in a breath and kept staring beyond Hudson's shoulder. "I know I screwed up big time."

"Screwed up what?" Hudson feigned ignorance. At least he could speak, having managed to swallow the potatoes, but his throat was closing. Everything was closing and closing in on him.

"I'd . . . No pressure. Okay?" Stephen flipped up his hand so his palm faced Hudson.

"Pressure about what?"

"Like I said, I screwed up big time. When we were kids." Stephen kept shoving the food around on his plate. "I know I should've stood up to my dad. I know that. But . . . he was the way he was." Begging was in his eyes. "I guess what I'm trying to say is I'd like us to . . . We're being friendlier than two people who, err . . ."

Hudson had to stop the scowl from forming on his face. Just as expected, Stephen would say everything but what he really felt. Nothing had changed.

"I screwed up and I'd like a second chance."

The words coming from Stephen whirled at Hudson like a category five snowstorm.

"But we can move slow. Very slow," Stephen quickly added. "At your pace. You're in charge."

Hudson almost fell from his chair. For once, Stephen had spoken from his heart. There was no beating around the bush. Okay, there'd been a wee bit of beating, but he wouldn't be Stephen Brandt if he'd failed to skim around the topic. What mattered was he'd found his courage to spit out what was pinging around inside his brain.

"If you feel it's not happening for you, go ahead and let me know if it's not working," Stephen also added, voice tight. He held his glass of water and kept pressing on it with his fingers.

For once, Hudson had the upper hand. He should be elated, dancing on the table and screaming at the top of his lungs because he now had the man who'd busted his heart sitting right in his palm. But fear crept up his spine. Sure, Stephen had managed to say what was on his mind, but when it came to retreating when the tough got going, at the eleventh hour he could be counted on to pull an about-face.

Could Hudson trust him?

Those five letters were bigger than the exams Hudson had to undertake to become a nurse practitioner. Wait, the ball was in his court. They could move at his pace. Wasn't this what he'd wanted from the get-go?

It was his turn to shove the meal around on his plate.

"I don't need a decision tonight. Okay?" Stephen laid his palm over the back of Hudson's hand, stopping him from pushing at the pork roast. "You go ahead and take your time. You let me know when you're ready to let me know."

"You don't want an answer right now?" Hudson couldn't help his shock.

"No." Stephen shook his head. "You tell me when you're good and ready. I'll . . . I'll let you think on it. No pressure." He moved his palm off the back of Hudson's hand. "I know dinner didn't go the way you expected, and it'd be wrong of me to stay now. I think it's best I leave and let you . . . think." He shoved back his chair.

The words *don't go* sat at the opening of Hudson's mouth.

CHAPTER FOURTEEN: AROUND AND AROUND

"Mr. Brandt, do you have time to talk?" Melinda clutched her books against her chest.

Stephen finished wiping down the whiteboard. He'd barely heard her small voice over the ringing of the school bell. He pivoted. "Of course. I always have time." He motioned at his desk. "Have a seat."

Melinda pulled one of the desks in the front row up to Stephen's desk. She didn't sit behind it but on top. A tendril of her iron-curled black hair fell in front of her dark eyes.

She'd been quiet at the meeting on Friday afternoon, simply staring at her hands. And it'd been the first time Tiffany had skipped out, who was a true champion of the two-spirit group.

"What can I do for you?" Naturally soft-spoken, he didn't have to muster a gentle voice. In fact, a few radio listeners had emailed him to state how they loved his soothing, dreamy tone that always lulled them to sleep while listening to his show.

Melinda kept licking her lips and *umming* while turning her head to the window and then back to the floor in front of the desk Stephen sat on. They were face to face, but she wouldn't focus on him.

"You know, talking about feelings can be difficult. It took me a long time to speak about what's going on in here." He tapped his chest.

She glanced up while fingering the beads on her bracelet. "You speak about how you feel now?"

"I try. At times I can't get the words out, and other times I finally find the nerve to say how I feel." *Like Saturday night.*

"What would you do if you really loved two people but they felt different about stuff?" She ran her nail down the front of her binder, leaving a scratch.

He squinted. Boy, she was close to naming *that* tune, because what she had going with Tiffany was impacting her family. Not her whole family. Just one person. Her dad. "What stuff do they feel different about?"

"My dad says I'm only fifteen and too young to get serious about . . . anyone." She lowered her gaze.

Her words were a punch to his gut. Dad had said the same thing eons ago, not because he'd believed Stephen was too young, but because of who he'd been running around with. He folded his arms. "He doesn't want you to date?"

"He never said I can't date . . ." She lowered her head again.

Words were so hard to say at such a young age. "Is this about Tiffany?"

Melinda nodded. She scratched at her binder some more. There were hearts on top, one bleeding into the *Melinda :hearts: Tiffany and Tiffany :hearts: Melinda*. "My dad, he doesn't like her."

Boy, again, could Stephen relate. "Has he asked you to stop being friends?"

She shook her head. "He just says I'm too young to be getting serious. But I feel like it's a lot more than what he's saying."

Something else Stephen could relate to, since he'd heard the same words spoken from his father's mouth.

"When the group first started, and you talked to us, you said your dad disapproved. Did he ever approve?" Hope was in her tiny gaze.

Yeah, after I moved away for school, started living my own life, and he didn't have to witness who I truly am. "He tried in his own way, but he never really accepted."

"Did he hate you?" She winced.

"No. He didn't hate me." Stephen's heart went out to her. She was at the same crossroads he'd faced in high school. "But I think he wished I wasn't gay." However, this conversation wasn't about him. "What did your dad say exactly?"

"He said he's okay if Tif and I are friends, but we shouldn't get serious. He said I'm too young to know what I want." Her head remained bowed. By the time they were done talking, she'd have the top of her binder scratched up.

Too young to fall in love. It was Stephen's turn to wince. "Too young to what exactly?" *Know that you're gay?*

"He thinks I'll outgrow it." She raised her head. Defiance flashed in her dark eyes.

Yes, the *you'll outgrow it* speech. He'd heard that one, too. "How do you feel?"

Her lower lip quivered. "I know I won't outgrow it."

That was a hopeful answer. She was firm in who she was, he noted. "Do you feel pressure from anyone else, besides your father?"

Melinda tucked a strand of hair behind her ear. "Tiffy . . . she, um . . ." Her face reddened. "This is dumb, isn't it? I can't believe I'm talking to my teacher—" She stood so fast her binder slipped from the desk and she caught it before it crashed to the floor.

Stephen's heartbeat quickened. "Melinda, please." His words came out urgent. "I'm here for you. I understand. I really do."

She stared at him, her gaze searching. Her throat shifted. "Your story . . . what you told us. It keeps going round and round in my head. I feel like . . ." She zeroed in on the whiteboard. "I feel like I have to make a decision, and I don't know what decision to make." Water filled her eyes.

"What's this pressure you feel exactly? Is Tiffany coercing you?" Stephen had a good hunch she was, and boy, could he understand the amount of anxiety Melinda was facing.

"She wants us to . . . My dad's such a . . ." A tear seeped from her right eye. "I don't know what to do."

He couldn't give her the *it'll be okay* spiel. No teenager wanted to hear that for an answer. "You know, the elders stress we don't have to make decisions right away for a reason."

"Yeah?" She didn't sound convinced, going by the dulling of her voice.

Of course she wasn't convinced. Teenagers wanted everything right here and right now. He'd been no different in high school. "Just remember when you do decide, do it for you. What you feel here." He tapped the left side of his chest.

He sure hadn't listened to his heart. If he had, he wouldn't be waiting on Hudson's decision since Saturday night.

"Is that how you make up your mind?"

He wet his lips. "In the past, I didn't. But now, I try to let my heart in on the decision, besides my head."

"Yeah, you sit in your head a lot, I noticed." She giggled.

At least she was laughing, and he chuckled, too. "Melinda, answers never come fast enough, and decisions are hard to make when you have a lot to consider. Please remember, you don't have to decide today, or even tomorrow. I'm waiting on an answer from someone, and this person has been considering my offer since Saturday night."

"Oh, you mean Mr. Suggashie?" She tilted her head.

Goodness, for such a young person, she sure was perceptive. He cleared his throat.

"I noticed he looks at you a lot when we're meeting." She giggled again and shrugged.

Stephen hadn't noticed Hudson staring his way when they

met with the kids for the two-spirit group.

Footsteps squeaked down the hall, which was strange because school had ended and they'd been sitting in his classroom talking for the last fifteen minutes. The squeaks stopped.

Tiffany poked her head inside. "There you are."

For a brief second, terror filled Melinda's eyes. She gaped at Stephen and then glanced to Tiffany. "Uh yeah, Mr. Brandt and I were going over a lesson."

Lesson? He wasn't her teacher. Boy, Melinda sucked at lying more than Stephen did.

"Later. And thanks, Mr. Brandt."

"Anytime," he called out to her as she left the classroom with Tiffany tugging on Melinda's arm.

He lowered his gaze. Yes, the two were exactly like him and Hudson.

On Friday, Hudson left the nursing station just as the night shift arrived. The two-spirit youth meeting had been postponed until Monday, by request of Mackenzie who had an appointment at the band office. That meant Stephen had time for dinner before going to the radio station building.

Hudson whipped out his cell phone and punched the button for Stephen's number. Maybe they could swing by the diner. Fear kept creeping along Hudson's spine, but he couldn't put off giving Stephen an answer any longer.

"Hello."

"Hey, it's me. Well, you probably already know that." Hudson forced a chuckle. "Did you have time for a quick dinner before you head to the radio station?"

"It's doable. Mom and I were only gonna have soup for supper."

"Great. I'll see you in a bit." Hudson got into his truck.

He'd eaten a light lunch, so a quarter-to-five supper shouldn't be too filling. Plus, he was dying for a cheeseburger and fries after he'd sworn off junk as part of his diet. But one bad meal wouldn't hurt. Or maybe it would? Last Saturday he'd eaten all the whipped potatoes after Stephen had left.

Why couldn't he be one of those people who didn't turn to food when upset or anxious?

If only the nursing station was in the heart of the reserve, he could walk more often, instead of having to take his truck to work. He steered the vehicle toward the main part of the community.

Since the weather remained colder than an iceberg floating about in the Arctic, nobody was around. Just vehicles passing him in the opposite direction. He pulled into the diner's lot where Stephen's SUV was already parked.

Although Hudson had donned his parka, winter boots, and heavy gloves, he dashed inside before the weather froze him into a snowman.

Stephen sat at one of the tables with a view of the road, empty other than the occasional truck rumbling by. Hudson removed his jacket and slid the parka on the back of the chair.

"Cold enough for you?" Stephen poured tea from the individual stainless-steel pot into his mug.

"I thought I might morph into Frosty." Hudson used his chin to point at the tea. "That sounds like an excellent idea." He called out to the waitress, "I'll have what he's having."

"Sure thing, Hudson," the waitress called back.

"By the way, what are you having?" Hudson eyed the tea, ready to snatch the mug and down a good gulp since Stephen was adding honey to the hot beverage.

"The special. Meat loaf. Mashed potatoes. And a side of greens. It comes with soup or salad."

"Hudson, did you want soup or salad?" The waitress hovered next to the swinging doors leading into the kitchen.

"What's the soup?"

"Beef barley."

"Soup for me." Hudson turned back to Stephen.

"Smart man. I can't get warm." Stephen's light chuckle was the finger-stroking laugh capable of kissing every inch of Hudson's skin. "I even brought the portable bathroom heater with me. The radio station's been too cold lately."

"That's because it used to be the ice shack." Hudson couldn't help his snicker. "Sounds like you need someone to keep you warm while you're on the air."

"Yeah? You have anyone in mind?" Stephen's dimples appeared to match his shy, boyish smile.

"Oh, I can think of a lot of gay men who'd be up for the task, but . . ." Hudson swallowed. There was his opening.

The waitress sauntered over.

There went Hudson's chance to speak up.

She set down the mug and the small teapot. "I'll get your soup."

"Thanks." At least having the tea on hand would give Hudson something to do while they talked. Maybe the arrival of his drink was a blessing.

"Err . . . but what?" Stephen ducked his head.

Hudson fumbled with the honey. He was twirling the dipper in the wrong direction, and not gathering any of the thick gooey sweetness. So much for blessings. "I guess you can't accept their . . . uh . . . their offers because you're . . ." He sucked in a helping of breath.

If you fuck me over for the second time, I'll slug you. " . . . you're already seeing someone."

Stephen's eyes popped wide.

Hudson finally added honey to his tea. He gripped the dipper. "Don't you —"

"We'll go slow," Stephen replied in a reassuring voice. "At your pace." Color returned to his deathly white skin,

116

plumping the red undertone to his bronze flesh.

"My pace." For once, Hudson would be in charge, instead of the silly puppy jumping up and down around the alpha dog. Not that Stephen was some dominant alpha. He simply had the upper hand between them because the jerk was always in control of his feelings.

Why couldn't Hudson possess that kind of control? To decide whether to give up his heart or not? Instead of his heart deciding the matter of its own accord?

He crossed his toes beneath his boots.

Please don't hurt me this time. Don't toss it all in my face like you did before.

CHAPTER FIFTEEN: CAUGHT UP IN YOU

"Are you going out?" Mom sat in her recliner. She had the TV on.

Stephen left the bedroom and leaned on the wall where the linen was stored. He had a full view of the living room from his vantage point since the tiny hallway led into his bedroom and the bathroom.

"Yeah. Fishing."

Mom's gaze drifted back to the TV. "Your father loved taking you ice fishing."

"I'll be back late afternoon. So don't worry about a ride to bingo." He returned to his room to finish dressing. "Are you doing anything today?"

"There's not much I can do, can I?" A hint of bitterness was in her reply.

Guilt flecked the back of Stephen's neck. He'd told himself many times not to feel responsible for her illness or the fact she wouldn't try an activity to fill her days. Maybe they should talk? Perhaps she should start taking responsibility for her condition? He had a right to build a life for himself.

"Are you going with Hudson?" Mom called out.

Stephen drew the sweater over his thermal undershirt. "Yeah."

Grumbling came from the living room.

He again left the bedroom. There wasn't anything to prepare. Hudson had insisted on packing some sandwiches, drinks, and coffee. All Stephen had left to do was get his equipment. "Are you gonna be okay?"

Not only did Mom have her illness to deal with, but she still mourned Dad.

"I'll be fine." She used her swollen fingers to pick up the toast in front of her on the TV tray.

Stephen winced. Because of her swollen joints, she wore her wedding, engagement, anniversary, and family rings around her neck on a chain. "Did you want me to get you anything on my way home?"

"No. I'll be fine. I'll warm some soup for supper. Did you want me to have anything prepared for you? You'll be due in at the radio station once you get back."

"A sandwich to go with the soup would be good. I got to get going. You have a good day. Okay, Mom?"

Her smile never reached her black eyes.

Stephen left the house, and much to his heartache, guilt followed him out the door.

Inside the pop-up fishing tent, Hudson poured himself another cup of coffee. It was the perfect day for ice fishing. Blue sky. Not a cloud present. But the caveat was a no overcast sky meant nothing contained the heat so there was a strong chill in the air. Even though they'd set up close to the shoreline hidden by a good helping of spruce trees, the cold kept trying to crawl inside his layers of clothing. They'd already unpacked the sleigh, drilled two holes in the ice, and sunk their lines. Occasionally, one of them approached the holes to jig their lures.

He shouldn't complain. Minus twenty-five Celsius was a welcome respite from the Jack Frost weather of minus thirty-five. The air was fresh on Hudson's tongue. He could've eaten what the Great Mother had sprinkled over the land this morning.

Even bundled up in his snow pants, parka, toque, and

dickie, Stephen was more delicious than pan-fried walleye, what Hudson hoped to cook once they'd nabbed a few from the frozen lake.

To protect their eyes from the bright sunlight on the pure-white snow, both had slipped on sunglasses.

"Too bad I'd freeze my dick. I sure could go for a blow job." Hudson snickered.

Stephen also chuckled.

Sex, although tempting if they snuck inside Hudson's truck, wasn't on the agenda. They had the morning and afternoon to spend together, an activity they'd engaged in numerous times in the past. And that was the pink elephant in the room—the past.

Stephen had asked for a clean slate to begin dating again. They had a fifteen-year gap to speak about, something they'd been avoiding.

"How'd you like living in southern Ontario?" Hudson sipped his coffee. He couldn't judge Stephen's reaction because of the black specs, but his jaw did stiffen slightly.

"It was okay. I guess." Stephen shrugged. His lips were redder and plumper from the cold weather.

"Tell me about it." Hudson had to know.

"There's not much to tell. I thought it was a good place to go after I got my teaching degree. Thunder Bay was . . ." Stephen folded his lips together. "I knew I needed to come out, and T. Bay wasn't the place to do it at the time."

Hudson sipped more coffee. "Southern Ontario was?"

"Yeah. More accepting. It helped me find my backbone. Dad had hidden it somewhere hard to find." Stephen's dimples appeared.

"You mean the nerve to also tell your parents finally?"

Stephen nodded. "I kept putting off dating, but I knew I had to get it together. That's when I met someone. He wasn't a teacher, but he did work for the board of education."

The color green was probably plastered all over Hudson's face. "Was he handsome?" He did his best to keep his question light. He was the one who'd voiced they had to discuss the past, after all.

"I don't think it really matters. I'm not with him, am I?" Stephen tilted his head slightly.

True. He wasn't. "Didn't work out?"

Stephen shrugged. "He was right for the time."

"Right?"

"He helped me with coming out. Accepting who I am. Realizing I couldn't carry my dad's baggage anymore."

"You mean how he felt about you being gay?"

"Yeah." Stephen wet his lips. "I can't be someone else just because someone I love wants me to. I gotta be me. The guy I dated helped me understand that. He also helped me realize how much I loved radio, and he said I should consider getting on with a station. Part-time, of course. I did when I moved to Thunder Bay. Not full station work. More like errand boy. But it made me realize why I became a teacher in the first place. I was still trying to follow in my father's footsteps."

"If you could pick becoming a full-time deejay over a teacher, would you?" Hudson held his breath.

"The reserve needs teachers." Stephen's smile was weaker than the cup of coffee Hudson had picked up at the diner the other morning.

"The rez will always need teachers. There's such thing as subs."

"I have my mom to support. I don't think an Internet radio station's going to pay the bills." Stephen opened the thermos and poured a refill into his mug. "Living up here is expensive. It's not like southern Ontario where everything you want is at your fingertips."

"She collects disability, doesn't she?" Hudson couldn't reveal confidential files at the nursing station, but he'd seen the letter from the doctor written up stating Mrs. Brandt's condition.

"It's not much." Stephen gazed out at their flat flags indicating no fish were biting. "She worked in social services for years. She knew the piddly amount she'd receive."

"But the house is paid for, isn't it?" The monthly payments for homes on the reserve weren't much either, not like the mortgages in a town or city.

"Yes, but propane is major money. My ride's almost all mine, though. Five more payments and it's no longer the bank's." Stephen finally fixed his coffee with cream and sugar. "The groceries and gas are also killer."

Hudson nodded. The propane, besides gasoline, was special fuel brought in on the plane. He made way more money than Stephen. Instead of falling under the provincial government that provided double the funding for public schools, which resulted in a great salary and pension for teachers, First Nations received a handful of peanuts from the federal government to operate their schools and pay their staff. And the staff weren't unionized like the provincial system. Hence why teachers were hard to come by on the reserves, especially isolated reserves.

Stifling his sigh, because Stephen would never achieve his true dream, Hudson forced back some coffee and let his gaze drift to their fishing holes. "You said the first guy helped you lots. What about boyfriend number two?"

Again, Stephen ducked his head. "Oh . . . well . . . it was . . . y'know. It was okay."

Hmm, the relationship had either been *that* bad or *that* good. Hudson prayed for the former. "What do you mean? Okay in what respect?"

Stephen kept his head ducked. "It started out okay. But, well, he wanted to get serious, and at the time, I wasn't looking for serious. I wasn't ready for serious." He lifted his head up, but the sunglasses continued to hide his eyes.

"Serious? You mean you wanted something sexual?" Hudson's heart hammered.

"No." Stephen's sunglasses moved a hint, meaning his eyes had widened. "I wanted us to date but not get serious."

"I see." Hmm, there was something else he was failing to say, Hudson noted. But he wouldn't press.

"What about you? You mentioned living with four guys," Stephen said quickly.

What a way to turn the tables. Hudson refrained from snorting. "I told you already, I had too much baggage and screwed up each relationship."

"The trust thing?"

Hudson nodded. "Yep, the trust thing."

"I feel . . . I'm sorry. So sorry. I know trusting someone is hard, and I really let you down. I cost you four great guys." Stephen's shoulders slumped.

"If they were so great, maybe they would've stuck it out longer. Persisted." Hudson rubbed his chin.

"Persisted?"

"You're persisting, aren't you? And you're not the persistent type." Becoming a teacher because his parents had wanted him to, throwing Hudson's love back in his face, everything about Stephen summed up the word persistent wasn't in his vocabulary — until now.

"I know trust is hard to reclaim if you broke trust before." Stephen again took an interest in their fishing lines basking under the bright light of the sun.

Hudson squirmed. Maybe it was time for him to get off the fence. "Isn't that why we're out here?" He removed his sunglasses. Being under the canvas kept the sun's bright rays reflecting off the white snow from stinging his eyes.

Stephen also removed his sunglasses. He stuck the end of the arm between his lips. The specs jiggled a bit, as if he was gnawing on the tip. "Yes."

"You want us to start over. Clean slate. I think that's what we're trying to do, instead of sucking each other's dicks . . . even though I'd give anything to suck yours right here and now." Hudson couldn't help his laugh.

Stephen also chuckled. "I think it'd freeze and fall off before you got your lips around it."

"So we're trying. I'm gonna admit I'm nervous. I keep thinking about when we were seventeen and it all screwed up." Hudson's knee bobbed.

"That's why I asked if we could start again. We're not seventeen anymore. We're not the same people." Stephen leaned in and rested his palm on Hudson's rattling knee, caressing it.

The stroke on Hudson's knee was full of tender care. Even reassurance. "You played *Caught Up in You* the other night. Was that a hint?"

"Maybe there're many hints if you listen closely." Stephen's blue eyes twinkled.

"You always preferred to let the music do the talking." Warmth filled Hudson, even though there wasn't a fire. The glowing ember stirring in his belly came from Stephen's tender gaze penetrating Hudson's skin. "I guess that's why I was asking you all those questions earlier. If I could give you your dream, I'd do it in a second."

"My dream?"

"Being a full-time deejay."

"Maybe it's another dream I want you to grant," Stephen murmured.

Hudson froze. Just then the flag popped up on Stephen's line. As for whether it was bad timing or perfect timing, Hudson wasn't sure. "You got one."

"I'd better go check it." Stephen's palm left Hudson's knee. He stood and tramped off to the fishing hole.

Hudson followed. Everything was in his court, even the

tennis racket, because he knew what dream Stephen was asking for.

Chapter Sixteen: Turnin' To You

Date number two. Jesse was filling in at the radio station for Hudson and Stephen's Wednesday night outing. Together, they'd ride the snowmobile trails and then stop at the diner for some food.

Hudson's nerves were a jumbled mess, all because he was on his way to retrieve Stephen at his place. No doubt Mrs. Brandt would be home. She hadn't given Hudson much of a warm welcome in the past, and tonight he'd see if her greeting was still icier than the teeth-chattering weather snaking through the reserve.

At least when they snowmobiled, they'd be hidden in the spruce forest instead of out on the open ice, keeping the wind at bay.

Along the way, Hudson kept up a chant of positivity. He hadn't been to the Seven Mile after he returned because there was no reason for him to travel to the area. As he drew closer to Stephen's place, his stomach tightened.

Up ahead was the three-bedroom home Hudson had visited in his youth, a mere walk to the school, the very place where he'd fallen in love.

He pulled into the driveway where Stephen's SUV was parked. Great. Stephen wasn't outside. Hudson sighed. Now he'd have to go inside and wonder how cold of a greeting he'd receive from Mrs. Brandt.

With no choice but to remove his helmet and shut off the snowmobile, Hudson stood and huffed to the side door. Before he lost his nerve and slunk off, he knocked.

Moments later, the last person Hudson wanted to meet stood before him.

Mrs. Brandt's thin lips remained in a straight line. "Hello. I'm so used to seeing you at the nursing station. It seems odd to see you anywhere else. Come in. Stephen's almost ready."

At least she'd stepped aside so Hudson could enter the utility room where the washer and dryer were located, along with the spot for coats and boots. The only change since he'd last been to the Brandts' residence was the propane furnace.

Mrs. Brandt folded her arms and assessed him up and down. Her left eye twitched.

Hudson stopped his body from wanting to shift from side to side, even though his feet yelled at him to move.

The tension grew thicker in the small room, almost suffocating. A cough rose in his throat that he stamped down. He firmly kept his chin high while staring back at Mrs. Brandt.

If his imagination had run amok, he'd liken their stare-off and silence as a contest of who'd break first.

A door shut. Footsteps padded along the carpet and then clomped along the floor. Hudson still held Mrs. Brandt's icy stare.

"Hey, sorry to keep you waiting. Mom had a last-minute chore for me to do." Stephen's voice seemed to pop the tension crowding the utility room. "They're all hung." He turned his attention to Mrs. Brandt.

"Thank you," Mrs. Brandt murmured, staring at her son. "I'll see you later." She left the utility room, closing the door.

Had there really been a chore Mrs. Brandt had needed her son to perform, or had she kept Stephen busy, leaving Hudson with no alternative but to come inside and face her frosty greeting? As for her not giving him a simple goodbye, that wasn't a big surprise either. At the nursing station, she always wore her mask of winter around him.

"Wow, I've met warmer snowmen." With that, Hudson

tossed open the door and stepped outside. His goose-pimpled skin thanked him for putting distance between him and the icicle Mrs. Brandt.

He stalked to the snowmobile just as the back door shut again. Footsteps banged on the steps clear of snow. No doubt Stephen was laying salt on the back entrance for his mother so she wouldn't slip and fall.

Hudson's old two-up machine still worked. In November, he'd taken the snowmobile to the reserve's best mechanic. After some tinkering, Joey had gotten the engine purring like a kitten at a saucer of milk.

Again, they'd be getting on the sled as they'd done as teenagers.

Stephen automatically knew his spot and slid on the back. Hudson took the driver's seat and started the engine. They were off. Instead of turning the machine around, he cut a path up the bank of the driveway and guided them across the blanket of thick snow on the lawn, took them across the ditch, and then onto the road.

Up ahead, there was a path leading into the spruce forest, a trail they'd taken in their youth that remained clear to this day. It was a spot at the Seven Mile where people liked to hike and snowshoe. Many also used it to snowmobile.

The machine roared down the road as Hudson aimed for the opening. They encountered a thud where the dip in the ditch was and bounced back up onto the narrow trail. Spruce boughs were arms reaching out to them.

There were lots of twists and turns to navigate that filled Hudson's lungs with excitement. He couldn't sense Stephen riding shotgun since there was plenty of room on the sled, and Stephen most likely was holding the arm rails, because the back seat rode higher than the driver's seat.

For forty-five minutes, Hudson took in nature at its finest with only the headlight of the snowmobile and the illumination from the moon to guide them. He drove them to the old campgrounds and back. The ride was as refreshing as a cold glass of water after trekking through the desert. Exhilarating. So alive.

He'd spent too much time in the city. Out here, at one with nature, his soul seemed to reach for the stars where his Ojibway ancestors lived. Too soon he was guiding them back to the opening of the trail. But they wouldn't go to Stephen's house. Hudson steered them to the fork in the road, straight for Main since they were grabbing a bite to eat at the diner.

At least Jesse had been eager to fill in for Stephen tonight, but there was a smidgen of guilt nagging Hudson. The radio station was Stephen's responsibility, even if Jesse enjoyed hosting. But if Stephen minded taking the night off, he didn't say so.

They arrived at the diner and seated themselves at a table by the window, Hudson's favorite spot so he could be nosy and watch the road. Maybe he was also a little proud to be seen? For so long he'd been a hermit. Although everyone knew they'd been best friends as teenagers, the community was aware they were both gay, which meant tongues were probably wagging. Something he didn't mind.

He set his helmet on the spare chair and removed his heavy coat. As for his snowmobile pants, those would have to remain on. Hopefully, he wouldn't get too hot.

"If I burst into flames from all these layers, I won't mind. She was a cold ride." Stephen rubbed his palms together. "I'm gonna get the wild rice soup and bannock."

Hudson would pass on the special he'd spied on the whiteboard when they'd first entered the diner. It was best he stick to his diet and forego the Salisbury steak served with pan fried mushrooms and gravy, mashed potatoes, and side of greens. "I'll get the same."

"You told me you were starving. I thought for sure you'd

have the special."

And be a pig? Screw it. Hudson would have the special. "You talked me into it."

Stephen's smile was on the shy side. "How about some tea?"

"I could use a warming up." The flirty words easily slid from Hudson's mouth. He didn't let his coy stare drift anywhere else either, but kept it pinned on Stephen.

The perfect shade of bashful pink spread across Stephen's face. "Is that an offer?"

"What do you think?" Hudson set his forearms on the table and leaned in.

"Then I'll take you up on it." Stephen withdrew his phone. "I hope this didn't freeze on our drive. I made sure and kept it in my shirt pocket." His eyes lit. "It's working. I was a bit worried. I gotta text Mom. Let her know I'll be late. I hope she wasn't expecting me to bring her something home."

The waitress sidled over and took their orders.

Once she returned with their teas, Hudson decided now was the best moment to speak about Stephen's mother. "I didn't get much of a greeting from her when I picked you up."

"From Mom?"

Hudson nodded. "She doesn't speak to me unless she has to if she's at the nursing station."

Stephen set his elbows on the table and rested his chin on his knuckles. "Unfortunately, Dad had a lot of influence over her."

"He still does, then?"

A frown creased Stephen's forehead. "Maybe it's time I talked to her."

Oh boy, it was that bad? Mrs. Brandt didn't dislike Hudson but hated him? He cleared his throat. "They never approved of me, did they?"

Stephen stared at the window just as a truck drove by.

Seconds passed before he glanced back to Hudson. "Their opinions differ from mine. Okay?"

Opinion? They did hate him. A flash of anger erupted in Hudson's chest. "What did I ever do to them?"

"You did nothing wrong." Stephen picked up his mug. "It's her problem. Not yours."

Great. Even with Mr. Brandt gone, he'd still found a way to make Hudson's life miserable. He gazed up at the outdated popcorn ceiling. There were so many hurdles in their path, one jump after another.

Dating was supposed to be fun, a getting-to-know-you period while building a potential relationship. But for them, they had too much baggage from yesterday, too many scars that would never fade.

Stephen's fingers clasped around Hudson's, and he jumped slightly. The searching gaze from across the table penetrated his chest.

"I know what you're thinking." Stephen's voice was quieter than his usual gentle tone. "I'm asking you to try."

"Try?" Hudson's teeth clattered. "She doesn't even like me."

"I understand. I do. I'd be disappointed if someone you loved didn't feel . . . well, didn't, err . . ."

"Say it. Didn't like me, right?" Hudson's eyes narrowed. "We got too many strikes against us. We can't undo the past. We can't undo—"

"No, we can't." Stephen's voice remained hushed. "But we can do our best to move ahead, can't we?"

"I guess so." Trying to remain indifferent was a big effort when Hudson's heart, the spot Stephen's words had touched, pleaded with him to climb over the table, wrap his arms around Stephen's shoulders, sit on his lap, and pretend Mount Everest they had to hike didn't exist.

"You guess so?" This time Stephen's voice firmed.

"I want to try again. I really do." Hudson licked his lips. "But if she doesn't approve of me, doesn't even like me . . . She's your mom. She needs you. She's the reason you moved back. Right? To care for her."

"Did you ever think I moved back for another reason?" Stephen's gaze altered to the chest-penetrating, intense stare that wormed its way into Hudson's heart.

"There was another reason?"

"Maybe I was tired of where I was living. Maybe I wanted to come back home. Maybe I realized living in the city wasn't where I was supposed to be. Maybe I came back to where I belong."

His eyes seemed to say *where you belong. Where we belong.* Or maybe Hudson's imagination had gone wild and his wishful thinking was dreaming up what he hoped lay in Stephen's heart.

"You feel this is where you belong?"

Stephen nodded. "What about you?"

Hudson belonged here, too. He belonged with Stephen. "Let's get our food to go. I want you."

"We can do that." Stephen squeezed Hudson's fingers.

"Then let's go. I know you gotta be home soon." Thanks to Mrs. Brandt, Stephen couldn't stay overnight. But maybe Hudson wasn't ready to have anyone sleep in his bed yet.

They were dating. Taking things slow. But as usual, his impatience was winning the game, wanting everything right here and right now, the very impatience that had caused them to crash and burn the first time around.

Chapter Seventeen: Hearts on Fire

Hudson almost tripped over a pair of boots he'd probably forgotten to store away as he continued to melt his mouth all over Stephen's. He hadn't bothered to throw another log on the fire once they'd arrived at the house. His greedy hands slid along the front side of Stephen's snow pants, and he copped a feel of his hard cock.

He plunged his tongue between Stephen's lips, tasting and exploring his slick flesh while having his mouth probed by Stephen's just as eager tongue.

Hudson wrenched the button to his snow pants open at the same time Stephen hurriedly unfastened his own. They tore at the layers of clothing, remaining locked at the lips, their mouths plastered as one while they bumped the wall to reach the bedroom.

Boy, one thing they were good at was fucking. And Hudson knew Stephen was attempting to get them past the humping stage. He wanted the same thing, but spending the night was a big move. Hudson had promised himself to take their shiny new relationship slow. Hell, if he asked, he'd get a *no* anyway, all because of their newest hurdle—Mrs. Brandt.

"I can't believe I'm thinking about your mother," Hudson muttered.

Stephen stiffened. "You're thinking about my mom?" His tone was incredulous.

"Never mind." Hudson wriggled from the last of his snow-mobile apparel. "It has to do with spending the night. I'm debating if I'm ready, but the point's moot since your mom will guilt you into going home." He laid his palms back over Stephen's bare ass, whose jeans pooled around his ankles.

Stephen kicked the denim material away. "Try me. If I get home early enough in the morning, it's good."

"Yeah?" Hudson plastered his lips back over Stephen's. "Then stay the night." His plea came out shaky.

"Gladly." Stephen's reply was hot in Hudson's mouth. "I never thought you'd ask. I wanna fuck you so bad."

The sultry declaration produced goosebumps along Hudson's spine. They were both naked, their bare flesh touching. He was pressed against the wall, with Stephen grinding his crotch along Hudson's hard dick. If they didn't get busy, he'd shoot his load everywhere.

Stephen broke the kiss, leaving Hudson to catch his breath through heavy gasps. He laid his head on the wall and let Stephen nibble on his earlobe. Stephen's smooth lips then shifted to Hudson's neck. Steam coated his skin from the sweet kisses painted on him. His spine was pure jelly, ready to dissolve onto the floor. He could have stood like this forever, letting Stephen explore every inch of his flesh with his mouth.

His body was wet and spongy, as if his limbs would slide to the floor where his spine was. No massage by the physical therapist who came to the nursing station every other week could beat the sultry kisses Stephen plied on Hudson's skin. Not only did his neck receive sensual pecks, so did his chest.

All he could do was lock his fingers into Stephen's thick black hair and moan. When his stomach received a tender peck, Hudson stiffened. He loathed the bulge he couldn't shuck, no matter how many salads he ate for lunch.

Maybe he'd stiffened, because Stephen softly said, "You're perfect. Absolutely perfect. I've never met a more perfect man than you."

The tender words coaxed away the self-consciousness shaming Hudson. "Yeah?" he whispered.

"Yeah," Stephen murmured while continuing to peck Hudson's gut. He even suckled the speckle of hairs circling his naval.

Hudson licked his lips. His skin burned hot with anticipation the longer Stephen continued to lick and kiss his lower stomach. The groans wouldn't stop leaving his mouth. His dick wouldn't stop flickering, waiting and wanting to fuck Stephen's mouth.

The lazy caresses Stephen showered all over Hudson's thighs left his skin tingling. He dug his fingers deeper into Stephen's scalp and grunted. That mouth was looking too delicious nibbling away at Hudson's flesh. Even the breaths of air coming from Stephen's nose were heaven on Hudson's skin.

The delicious tender kisses formed a path from Hudson's naval to his crotch.

When Stephen buried his face into Hudson's groin and sniffed, a shock of electrical excitement surged up Hudson's spine, and he thrust his hips. He didn't stop wiggling about until his cock brushed Stephen's lips.

"Take it," he panted. "C'mon. Take it." Fuck, he was being tortured. He still had a hold of Stephen's hair and guided his head to his cock.

"Forcing me?" Stephen's hot words caressed Hudson's erection.

"Damned straight. Take it or I'll shove it into your mouth." There was a growl to Hudson's words.

"What if I don't?" Taunting filled Stephen's reply.

"Oh, you will." Hudson couldn't help his snicker. "You'll take it all. Every damn inch."

"How many inches?"

"More than you can handle." Hudson used his free hand to rub the head of his dick along Stephen's mouth. "Suck it."

"Hah, I can more than handle it. I handled it before and I'll handle it again." Mischievousness sparkled in Stephen's glimmering gaze.

Just as Hudson was about to make a snappy comeback, his prick was immersed in slick, wet heat tantalizing enough to tease every inch of his body. He sighed and again found his head against the wall while he kept his hand in Stephen's hair. With a gentle tug, he urged Stephen to take more until Hudson's full length was coated with saliva and tasting pure heaven.

He released Stephen's hair and cupped the back of his head. With a grunt, Hudson rocked his hips back and forth, thrusting his cock in a quick rhythm between Stephen's sucking lips. The smacking and *mmms* coming from Stephen toyed with Hudson's senses, where he was close to exploding.

All he could do was keep fucking and enjoying the moment.

When Stephen's finger penetrated Hudson's asshole and wiggled along his inner flesh, the euphoria running through his limbs shattered into a million pieces. He had to grip the wall to stop from sliding down as the release continued to pulsate through him.

He couldn't stop panting or licking the air, holding tight to the sensual sensations continuing to claw at his skin. His heart kept hammering, and his fingers remained in Stephen's hair.

"I want you." Hudson gasped. "In me. Now, man."

Stephen rose. A dribble of cum was at the corner of his mouth. He slathered his lips over Hudson's, giving him a taste of the milky jizz that he'd released moments ago.

"One second," Stephen murmured. He disappeared inside Hudson's bedroom that they'd never made it to.

Hudson continued to catch his breath. Seconds later, Stephen appeared holding the tube of lube. Hudson was spun around to face the wall. His legs were shoved apart and Stephen's heated breath was on the back of his neck, along with his taunt, "I'm gonna fuck you good and hard."

Being roughly manhandled left Hudson shivering.

Stephen rested his palms on Hudson's stomach. His cheeks were spread by what he'd ached for ever since they'd entered the house. He held his breath, burning with anticipation. The head of Stephen's prick was enclosed between Hudson's buttocks and it began to slowly breech him. Hudson pressed his forehead on the wall, his heart tightening. Finally, the rest of Stephen's length slid inside. Full. Pure bliss and a nick of pain enveloped Hudson. He set his hands on the wall for leverage and raised his ass higher.

The pumps started slow, just enough to stretch and tease him. He couldn't help flexing his ass cheeks, squeezing Stephen's cock that moved in and out.

"You feel so good," Stephen murmured into Hudson's ear. "So good."

"You feel good," Hudson whispered back. He squeezed again.

"More. Squeeze some more." Urgency claimed Stephen's order.

Hudson obeyed and tightened his asshole. The thrusting came faster and deeper. He was close to being split in two, and his heart wouldn't stop banging, sending excitement coursing through his veins.

He loved being the one to make Stephen come. He loved being the one responsible for Stephen's lust.

Hudson curled his fingers into fists, close to banging on the wall. He gritted his teeth and took the pounding his ass was undergoing. He wasn't sure how much longer he could hold out when Stephen stiffened. His moans and gasps stroked Hudson's ears.

Quiet satisfaction coaxed Hudson's lips into a big smile. He'd made Stephen come . . . again.

Hudson lay in the pit of Stephen's arm and trailed his fingers down tight abs, the skin smooth to the touch. He was so content, not even a pillow curled up in a flannel case was cozier than him. Unable to resist, he brushed his toe along Stephen's calf.

"I want you again," Stephen whispered.

"Yeah?" Hudson craned his neck to gaze up at Stephen. "Me, too."

Stephen shifted, so Hudson uncurled himself from around the sexy limbs he was hugging and the gorgeous chest where his head rested. "How and where do you want me?" He snickered.

"All fours." Stephen cocked his brow.

Almost smirking, Hudson easily moved onto his knees and rested his palms in the comforter. "I'm the nurse practitioner. Shouldn't I be the one examining your prostate?"

Stephen smacked Hudson's ass. "A urologist does that, not a nurse practitioner."

"Okay. I'll let you be my urologist." Hudson couldn't resist peeking over his shoulder at Stephen licking his lips. "You look hungry. Like you're ready to eat."

"Maybe I am."

Stephen's declaration easily caressed Hudson's skin and touched him in his most intimate regions. "Then eat away."

"You mean like Sunday dinner?" Stephen kept caressing Hudson's ass. "I want you to join Mom and me."

Hudson stiffened. He wasn't ready to go there yet. The woman was colder than the temperature outside.

"Say yes, or I'll go to sleep." There was teasing in Stephen's warning.

"Seriously? You're blackmailing me?" Normally, Hudson would be annoyed, but for some reason, he laughed.

"Yes. Blackmail." Stephen leaned in and brushed his lips on Hudson's ass.

Hudson shivered and almost choked on his breath. "Damn you," he said through clenched teeth. "What a way to make me say yes."

"So it's a yes, is it? Sunday at two?" Stephen pecked the other cheek.

"Yeah. Now get busy. Eating, that is." Hudson kept peeking at Stephen over his shoulder.

"Mmm . . ." Stephen kissed Hudson's cheek again. "You don't need to ask."

Hudson faced the headboard. His ass was spread apart, and the touch of air slid between his cheeks. He held his breath, but nothing happened, because Stephen was still exploring Hudson's buttocks with his lips.

The kisses left Hudson gasping the closer those sexy lips neared his cleft. He wasn't sure if he should holler a *hurry up and eat* or just enjoy the sensual exploration the skin of both butt cheeks were enjoying. Still, being teased was maddening and tested his patience. Finally, what he yearned for happened. Stephen's tongue licked at the edge of Hudson's crack, leaving a path of saliva all the way to his hole.

Their intimate talk, the sex, even the snowmobile ride together was deep in Hudson's heart. He'd wanted to take it slow, but at this point, the love he tried to deny was knocking at the door, demanding to enter.

He curled his fingers into the comforter, panting from Stephen's tongue flicking and slapping at his hole. Nobody could rim like Stephen. Hudson's cock twitched. Hard. He was ready to be sucked off or jacked for a second time.

Not only did his cleft receive a licking, so did his balls. By the sweet *mmm*s coming from Stephen, he was enjoying himself. He must've been, because he buried his lips deep between Hudson's cheeks while still licking but also kissing in the most suggestive fashion, making out with Hudson's asshole as if he was kissing him.

Hudson shivered. The tip of his cock wouldn't stop throbbing. He needed to be touched, besides eaten.

He wiggled his buttocks in suggestion. The licks and saliva all over his hole was creating the most euphoric sensations. Stephen massaged Hudson's buttocks with sensual caresses sassy enough to wheedle him into complete submission as he bowed his head and groaned.

Dating. He'd agreed to try, but he couldn't deny what Stephen was doing to him, besides his tongue coaxing Hudson to give up his cum. He was deeply in love again. Deeply in love with the man who'd captured his heart over fifteen years ago, and there wasn't a damned thing he could do about it, other than say with a low hiss, "Jerk it. Jerk me."

Stephen's hand snaked beneath Hudson and encircled his cock. Being gripped was all it took. Rocking back and forth to fuck Stephen's face, Hudson thrust his cock deep into Stephen's fist.

The pleasure was coasting along Hudson's spine, ready to explode into pure pleasure. He let his body take full control and reached for the tantalizing euphoria he could almost taste.

When Stephen's tongue slid up and inside Hudson, the wiggling wet flesh swirling around his insides was all that it took for him to shoot his load.

CHAPTER EIGHTEEN: MAKE SOME SENSE OF IT

For fuck sakes. I'm in love.
Hudson curled his fingers into a fist and punched his reflection staring back at him. There was no denying who had his heart again, no matter how he'd tried to hold tight to the treacherous thing.

He had to be deeply, madly in love, because he was on his way to Stephen's house for Sunday dinner, after spending the week thinking about him, listening to his voice on the radio, and dreaming about a future that didn't include Mrs. Brandt.

For the ice queen, Hudson had baked a bannock for their meal. That way, Mrs. Brandt couldn't call him unthoughtful or rude for not bringing something.

Okay, he was set to go. There was no point staring at his round face in the mirror any longer. He spritzed on the cologne Stephen had bought him and left for the Brandt residence.

He made the drive in record time and pulled up at the house at two o'clock sharp. When he stood at the back entrance, he held his knuckles in the air, ready to knock with the bannock in the crook of his free arm. The same doubtful thoughts resurfaced.

I'm in love. But I can't do this. I can't go inside and pretend I like her when I know she doesn't like me.

Before he could change his mind and dash for his truck, he gave three sharp raps on the wooden door. At the sight of Stephen standing on the other side, the heartbeat and breath

Hudson held tight relaxed

"Hey. C'mon in." The bright sunlight reflecting off the snow was dull compared to the sparkle in Stephen's eyes.

"Hey, you're a real pro at this now. I'd say after what I tasted, you're a front runner for the stuff your grandma used to make." Stephen eyed the bannock. "Take off your boots. Your coat . . ." He leaned in, murmuring, " . . . and anything else you want."

What a tempting invitation. Hudson elbowed Stephen. "Yeah right. C'mon, I'm trying to get on your mom's good side."

"There's no good side to get on." Stephen's lips brushed Hudson's cheek. "What's not to like about you?" He motioned at Hudson to follow him to the kitchen.

Hudson trailed in his wake. He glanced to where Mrs. Brandt sat in a recliner. A shiver juddered down his spine. It'd been well over fifteen years since he'd last been inside the house. Except for new shaker-style white cupboards, stainless-steel appliances, smokey plank flooring, and the updated sectional, he could've been fifteen years old walking into the Brandts' home.

The TV was on.

He still clutched the bannock. "Hello. For you." He held out the bread wrapped in wax paper.

Mrs. Brandt nodded, but her smile was colder than the ice water running through her veins. No wonder her joints were constantly stiff. There was nothing to heat them up, like warm blood every normal person possessed.

Stephen strode to the stove. "I'm making pork chops and scalloped potatoes."

"Sounds good." Since Mrs. Brandt hadn't acknowledged the bannock Hudson still held, he ambled over to the range where Stephen stood with the oven door open, checking on the meal.

"Where did you want me to put this?"

"The counter's fine." Warmth radiated in Stephen's voice. He shut the oven door and straightened.

The things a guy does because he's dumb enough to let himself fall in love again. Don't let me regret this. Hudson set the bannock on the updated butcher block counter that had a walnut finish to match the floors.

Even though people were doing away with wall-to-wall carpeting, the Brandt home still had the stuff. The foam under the carpet was probably easier on Mrs. Brandt's feet—the joints on her soles were deeply swollen.

The table was already set. With Stephen having the dinner under control, Hudson had nothing to do but join Mrs. Brandt. He almost shuddered.

"There's juice in the fridge. Help yourself." Stephen had unwrapped the bannock. "And take a seat. I'm almost done."

"Sure," Hudson mumbled. He poured himself a glass, forced himself to beeline across the way to the living room, and sat on the edge of the sectional.

Mrs. Brandt stared ahead at the TV, squinting. Her interest in the commercial didn't fool Hudson. Who cared about hemorrhoid cream? He couldn't even get his own patients interested in caring for the problem around their anuses, let alone a woman who'd never spoken about having those itchy, pesky irritants on her bottom whenever she came to see him.

This was Stephen's mother, so Hudson had better play nice. "How you been?" he asked, although he'd seen her at the nursing station on Wednesday.

"Fine." Her voice was cooler than the juice Hudson held.

Why don't you like me? What have I ever done to you to earn your contempt? He swirled the ice in his glass.

Her finger braces she was supposed to wear whenever she wasn't busy with her hands sat unused on the side table. She probably didn't even wear them to bed. Sure, he could understand losing her husband two years ago wasn't easy. From what Hudson knew, she'd depended on Mr. Brandt to help her since she wouldn't allow any of the homemakers in the house, but she had to at least try. The only thing stopping her from being independent was herself.

She was sneaking a peek from the corner of her eye.

He cleared his throat. Shit, he hadn't noticed he was staring.

"Is there something you wanted to tell me?" Her question matched the sternness in her hard gaze.

The debate was on — whether to speak his mind or keep his trap shut. He swallowed. They were dating. Now that Hudson knew he was in love, he wasn't going anywhere. She had to accept him. He wasn't asking to be her best buddy, but at least he could be shown respect. That was the deal breaker. Before he confronted her, he should speak to Stephen first and let him know his mother's silent animosity had to stop.

"Dinner's ready," Stephen announced. He remained in the kitchen, grinning, and motioned at the table.

Hudson stood. He trounced to the chair Stephen held out. The meal smelled delicious, and it'd been eons since Hudson had last eaten scalloped potatoes. Like hell Mrs. Brandt was going to ruin Sunday dinner for him.

Stephen moved back to the counter. He had the pork chops on a platter that he placed on the table.

Mrs. Brandt had a special recliner designed to assist her with rising from the chair. She only used the cane when active and shuffled to the table. Stephen was readying a plate, cutting the pork chop into bite-sized pieces.

The woman was only fifty-nine, from what Hudson could remember on her chart. She was perfectly capable of manipulating the cutlery. He had to stop himself from huffing out an annoyed breath.

"I'll be seeing you at the nursing station for your session this week," Hudson said. Maybe she'd get the hint.

Mrs. Brandt shrugged. "I don't know why the specialist insists I continue with the sessions. They're not helping."

They're not helping because you're not trying. Hudson had to stop himself from grunting.

"I know it's because of the high levels of CRP and RF in my blood." She spoke quietly.

"The elevated levels you have in your blood may not be common, but the specialist has addressed this, according to your file." Hudson stabbed a pork chop from the platter.

"I'm tired of all the medications. The prednisone gives me too many mood swings."

Stephen sat. He dished up scalloped potatoes, as if there was nothing wrong with Mrs. Brandt's complaining.

Hudson eyed him. He had to stop himself from asking, *is she taking her meds on a regular basis? She'd better be, and you'd better make sure she is. Quit babying her. In the twenty-first century, RA is more than manageable. It isn't the crippled, deformed life sentence it once was when your kokum had it.*

Stephen never glanced Hudson's way. He was piling vegetables onto his plate.

"At times I wish I was with your father," Mrs. Brandt muttered, staring blankly at her plate she'd never thanked her son for attending to.

Hudson almost sputtered aloud. What a thing to say in front of a guest. As for Stephen, he was cutting up his own pork chop. "Have you thought about counseling?"

Mrs. Brandt's nose wrinkled, and her dark eyes scrunched. "Counseling? For what?"

You got done telling me you want to join Mr. Brandt in the grave. "I'm sorry, but you mentioned not . . . err . . . wanting to be here."

"Mom . . ." Stephen finally stopped fussing with his food. He gazed at her. "Can we just eat, please?"

Mrs. Brandt huffed. "Wait till you end up with RA." She almost pointed her fork at his face.

"I don't know if I will or won't, but the cards aren't in my favor, are they? From what Hudson told me, it isn't the disease it was when Grandma had it." Stephen's voice was firm but also soft.

Hudson almost cheered.

Stephen slipped some pork between his lips and continued to gaze at his mother. "I'm not going to worry about it. If it happens, it happens."

Mrs. Brandt shook her head. "I never expected you to understand. Nobody understands."

Biting down on his lip, Hudson cut a piece of pork and filled his mouth before he said something he'd regret.

"Mom, can we please eat." There was begging in Stephen's words.

Mrs. Brandt half harumphed and then sighed. She dug into her meal. "The pork's not tender enough."

For crying out loud, did this woman have to complain about everything? Hudson almost threw his fork on his plate. If he had to spend two hours listening to someone feel sorry for themselves and find fault with everything, he was out of here. She was doing this for his benefit. If she didn't want him here, why didn't she simply say so?

"If it's my presence that's causing—"

"It's fine," Stephen reassured him. He directed his attention at his mother. "We have a guest."

"I'm not going to pretend I'm fine." Mrs. Brandt huffed. "I'm in pain, and I'm not feeling well."

"If you're not feeling well and you're in pain, I'll come back another day." Hudson tossed aside his napkin and pushed back his chair. He stood. "If you don't want me here, just say it." He stared down at Mrs. Brandt.

A strange noise came from Stephen, but Hudson never spared him a peek. He continued to stare at Mrs. Brandt, who kept her icy eyes straight ahead, with her shoulders back and chin raised.

"Thanks for the meal." Hudson turned and marched for the utility room to retrieve his coat and boots. He had to admit the woman would never like him, much less approve of him, or even tolerate him.

While he donned his outerwear, nothing came from the kitchen. He slipped on his gloves. Just as he threw open the door and stepped outside, footsteps padded across the floor.

He shut the door anyway and tromped down the steps.

The back door opened.

"Can you wait a second?" Stephen called out.

Hudson swiveled and glared.

Stephen motored down the stairs, boots untied and minus his coat. He rubbed his bare arms against the cold. "I'm sorry. She hasn't been herself after Dad died."

"This is more than your dad. Face it. Your parents never liked me. And she still doesn't." Hudson couldn't help the bitterness in his words. "This is why you walked away the first time? It was because of them, wasn't it? Not because you were afraid of my love." He thrust his finger at the house.

"It didn't have to do with them. Okay?" Stephen brushed at his hair. Gooseflesh was forming on his bare arms. He rubbed his biceps. "I'll talk to her. I'll —"

"There's no point in saying anything." Hudson smacked his thigh. The frustration coiling through him was creating a thick ball of tension at the back of his neck. "Face it. We were never meant to be together, and it's because of your parents. If you'd finally admit it to yourself —"

"If you'd please listen to me —" Pleading surfaced in Stephen's eyes.

"What's there to listen to?" Hudson almost spit in the snow at his feet. "Y'know, never mind this dating bullshit." He held up his hands. "I know where this is going. And I don't want a repeat of last time. It took me a fuck of a long time to get over you."

He whipped on his heel and fished his keys from his parka pocket. "Have a nice life."

"Will you please listen to me?"

Shock peppered Hudson's skin. Usually, Stephen gave up and retreated. He wasn't a persistent man. Hudson pivoted.

"Is this really what you want?" Stephen's gaze searched Hudson's.

Hudson swallowed. No, it wasn't what he wanted, but he had no choice. To keep his sanity intact, and his heart in one piece, he had to leave.

He nodded. "Yeah. It is. I don't want to go through that kind of pain again." He got into his truck.

This time, Stephen didn't stop Hudson.

Through the windshield, Hudson watched Stephen stalk back to the house, taking a swipe at the air.

Chapter Nineteen: The Love That I've Lost

For two weeks, Stephen had thrown himself into work and deejaying. As for the twice-weekly two-spirit youth group meetings, Hudson had been a no-show. When the kids had asked about him, Stephen was forced to make excuses.

If not for the big crack in his heart, annoyance would've consumed Stephen. The kids needed Hudson. Just because they were at odds didn't mean the two-spirit youth should pay.

He'd also passed on dedicating anything to Hudson on the radio. They'd tried and had hit the wall with a big splat. Seeing Tiffany and Miranda twice a week reaffirmed they were as doomed as he and Hudson had been, which bothered Stephen more than it should have, but he didn't want to witness the girls experiencing the same heartbreak and resentment. He couldn't speak to them, though, because he was the worst example to use, unable to get his shit together and maintain a relationship.

Instead of being cheerful now that Hudson was out of the picture, Mom had become more withdrawn. She was in her recliner, staring at the morning news on TV while Stephen cooked breakfast before he left for the school.

He'd already come out and asked why Mom disliked Hudson, and she'd given her answer, so there was no point in asking again. Stephen didn't see the same traits in Hudson that Dad had possessed. At least Hudson was willing to listen, unlike Dad who'd been of the motto of *my way or no way.*

Mom stood. She shuffled to the kitchen. "Let me help."

Surprise shocked Stephen's system. She wanted to try? Seriously?

Mom took the knife from him. When she gripped the handle, her mouth formed into a firm line, and her brows wrinkled. She attempted a first chop at the onion for the pan fries.

Stephen made himself stay in his spot and not reach out to help her, even though every fiber of his being loathed witnessing her pain. He'd witnessed enough of her inner pain after losing Dad, helpless, unable to do anything to take away the loss she was suffering.

Words never came either. He hadn't been able to get her to talk about Dad's death, so there wasn't a chance he'd get through to her about why she wanted to help this morning. Hudson was right. Stephen almost sighed. He could never transfer what was happening in his mind to come out of his mouth. The only thing he did great was talk about music on the radio with other die-hards who phoned in, requesting he spin their fave song.

"What are you playing tonight?" Mom kept wincing but never stopped chopping. She set down the knife and gazed at the ceiling. "Do me a favor and get me one of my pills."

Stephen couldn't move fast enough to open the cupboard door where he kept her weekly pill organizer Mom forever ignored. "I'm doing a run of glam rock."

"You'd like to do that full-time, wouldn't you?" She took the pill from him. Her gaze searched his.

More surprise pinged and ponged through Stephen's limbs. She hadn't asked him anything about his life after Dad had died. He shrugged. "I'm a teacher."

She began chopping the potatoes. "I think we both know your father was responsible for that."

"The kids need me." He leaned his butt against the top of

the table and folded his arms.

"I guess what I'm trying to say is . . ." The knife in Mom's hand trembled.

Stephen pressed his lips together.

Was this why he kept everything upstairs, wrapped like an unwanted gift in his head? Mom was the same way, too. Ever since Dad had died, the house was too quiet, because Dad was their talker, the one to instigate and lead conversations.

"You don't have to keep teaching for my benefit. We'll manage. We'll get by." Mom continued to wince as she cut the last of the potatoes. "I have to start listening to my physio-therapist and the doctor. I've . . . I've pitied myself too long with this disease."

"It's okay. I understand." Stephen straightened. "Why do you think I came home?" He placed his hands on her shoulders.

"I know I haven't been easy to live with, but after Sunday dinner . . ." She dropped her head. "I'm sorry. I really am. I . . . I guess . . . you have your life to live." She lifted her head, staring straight at the cupboards.

"What do you mean?" He squeezed her shoulders.

"Your own life. Go to him." She took in a big breath and kept her chin straight.

"Go to him?" Stephen blanched. "I don't think—"

"You're too much like me." Mom sighed. "If you want to see him, go to him. Demand what you want. Maybe it's what he's hoping you'll do."

Hudson? Hoping Stephen would beg for a third chance? He'd barely gotten a second chance. But Mom was right. He was forever tucking his tail between his legs and returning to his doghouse to hide.

To brighten his Monday morning at the nursing station after

two weeks of misery, a trip to Winnipeg was on Hudson's agenda. He'd better get plenty of loonies and toonies to tip the strippers with. What a life. He rubbed his brow.

Mrs. Brandt's name jumped off the computer screen for his patient schedule. Right after lunch he'd see her. He tossed his pen on the desk. This was the worst way to start the week, so a trip to the city on Friday was something he desperately needed. But anticipating ten lap dances couldn't wipe the fact he'd have to face the woman in four and a half hours, who'd probably show up with a smug smile, having gotten her way.

Earlier, one of the elders had smudged the building, some-thing they did at the start of each week to cleanse the atmos-phere of negative energy and allow for positive vibrations not only for the staff but patients. The pessimism simmering in Hudson's blood didn't sit well with him. The lingering aroma of sage, burned in the abalone shell and dispersed by the elder with an eagle feather, was a reminder to follow the seven teachings of the seven Grandfathers.

He slumped in the chair.

Maybe he'd been too hard on Mrs. Brandt. Two years ago, she'd lost her husband, hardly enough time to mourn some-one. Not only had she'd lost her husband, but Mr. Brandt had been her primary caregiver. Everyone reacted differently to death and disease. Perhaps he should be more sympathetic to her plight?

Still, the thought of seeing her was too much for a Monday.

For three and a half hours, he threw himself into his work, seeing patient after patient. Because he was running late, when the clock struck noon, he scarfed down a sandwich and water at his desk while catching up on his paperwork. Then one o'clock arrived.

He was on time, having done his best to keep to schedule since he loathed forcing patients to sit forever in the waiting room. From what he stared at on the computer screen, the RN had already taken Mrs. Brandt's blood pressure. He buzzed the RN to let her know Mrs. Brandt could come in.

Within seconds the door swung open, and Mrs. Brandt followed the nurse inside.

Hudson swiveled his chair to give Stephen's mother his undivided attention. Mrs. Brandt sat in the opposite chair, her skinny fingers with the thick joints twisted around the strap of her purse.

"Before we start, there's something I'd like to say to you." For once, icicles didn't dangle from her words.

Shock kicked Hudson in the backside, and he leaned forward. "Oh? Is there something concerning you?" He used his most professional voice.

"I . . ." She kept wrapping the purse strap around her fingers. "I owe you an apology."

No matter how hard Hudson tried, he couldn't stop his mouth from falling open.

"I know I haven't been nice to you." She cleared her throat and glanced around the small office. Her gaze rested on the exam table.

He followed where she stared at the cushioned bed where patients laid or sat if required for their visit.

"I . . . I ruined our Sunday dinner." She cleared her throat. "I . . . I could be a better follower of the *red road*."

Hudson stiffened. He'd never heard the Brandts speak about Ojibway tradition. Not in his presence. Probably because Mr. Brandt had been as Canadian as poutine. He had a hunch Stephen's father had only resided up here for Mrs. Brandt's sake, since this was where her family lived—two brothers, a sister, and their children, and now grandchildren.

"It's time I started behaving how an *Anishinaabe-kwe* should behave." She coughed into her fist. "I was raised in a traditional family but . . . well, after marrying Brad . . ." She shrugged. "I've been hiding out at home for too long."

The loneliness in her stuttering words melted the top layer coating Hudson's frozen heart she'd turned to ice after the disastrous Sunday meal.

" . . . blaming everyone for my predicament, when every-one did their best to try and help." She kept twisting the strap around her fingers. "I won't get into specifics, but I wanted to say I had no right taking it out on you. Stephen likes you very much." She held up her swollen hand, palm facing him. "And don't think he sent his mother here to put in a good word for him. He has no idea what I'm doing, but I know he misses you."

Her words were a punch to Hudson's gut. Then if Stephen missed him so much, why didn't he say so? Fine, he hadn't sent his mom here to beg for a second chance, but cell phones existed. How hard was it to dial Hudson's number? It wasn't like the tower had gone on the fritz again. And landlines existed.

"This is all my fault. I know. I know." She held up her hand again. "Stephen's a grown man. He can speak for himself, but . . ." She let her purse slip to the floor. "I did more than my fair share of guilting him." She glanced away. "Truly guilting him that he was all I had now that Brad's gone."

Hudson nodded. Of course Stephen was torn between the woman who'd birthed him and was sick and alone, and the man who . . . *I love him. I miss him.*

But there was nothing Hudson could say. This was Stephen's fight. But when had Stephen ever fought? He always bowed to whatever his parents had asked of him and still did.

"Apology accepted." Hudson used his warmest voice, even though the ice had once again coated his heart. "As you said, Stephen's a grown man. If he wishes to speak to me, he has my number."

Stephen kept staring at his cell phone. The two-spirit students had left after a positive meeting, or so it seemed since Melinda and Tiffany had held hands during their round table discussion.

Footsteps pattered down the hall. The noise grew closer and stopped at his classroom. Still holding his cell phone, Stephen glanced up to Melinda hovering in the doorway.

"I thought you left with Tiffany. What can I do for you?" Stephen set aside his cell phone.

Feet dragging, Melinda entered the classroom. She meandered to the desk across from his and plopped in the seat. By her downcast gaze and twiddling her thumbs, something had upset her.

"Everything okay?" Stephen used his warmest tone.

"It *was.*" Melinda shrugged. "Tiffany wants us to go to the dance together."

"She asked you to the dance? Just now?" The dance was occurring next Friday. Stephen would deejay while Jesse broadcasted the show.

Melinda nodded.

"And this bothers you?"

"Yeah. It's cool when we're here, talking to you. But doing it in front of everyone makes me nervous."

"Doing what?"

"Like dancing." She shrugged. "What if everyone laughs at us? What if I make my dad even madder? What if he finds out we were dancing together?"

Those were tough questions, and Stephen reminded himself he was a teacher. He couldn't give specific answers that might interfere with her home life. Plus, she had to find the answers for herself. "Melinda . . ." He made sure his gaze was as kind as his voice. "Have you talked to your mother?"

"I told you, she lets him push her around." Melinda's eyes flashed. "He's so bossy. It's always gotta be his way."

Boy, that sounded familiar. "Let's tackle the dance first. You mentioned people laughing at you. Dancing together. But you have the courage to come to the two-spirit meetings."

"Well, yeah. It's different here." The face she made was one of *duh, don't you get it?*

"Safer, maybe?" He arched his brow.

Pink spread across her cheeks. "Um . . . I guess so." She lowered her head and stared at the top of the desk. "You can always read my mind." Her words were muffled.

"This may be hard to believe, but I was a teenager once, too." He used his most coaxing voice.

She lifted her head. Her stare was true to what every fifteen-year-old believed — nobody over thirty had ever been young.

He almost laughed, because he'd shared the same thoughts when talking to his old mentor, Mr. Petersson. At seventeen, Stephen had been unable to fathom anyone thirty and older as a kid. "Times were a bit different then. Not *that* different, but a bit different."

"Did your parents accept you?" She drew a line across the top of the desk.

"It doesn't really matter who accepted me. What matters is you, and how you feel. You said you don't feel comfortable about going to the dance with Tiffany. What you have to figure out is why."

"I told you. People will tell my dad, and he'll get mad."

"So you don't mind dancing with her in front of others?"

Pink reappeared on her cheeks.

"You know, people are people. That's why I started our group. So each one of you understand we are people first."

"Easy to say." She shrugged again. "But it's different when your dad isn't cool with it."

"I know you tried to talk to your mom. Is there anyone else in your family you can talk to?"

"Not really. I don't think anyone would understand."

"You won't know unless you try."

"It's . . ." She stood and glanced around. "It's just too complicated."

"Have you tried talking to Tiffany about how you feel?"

"You know the answer to that." She sniffed.

"I know it's hard when your partner doesn't want to hear your true feelings, but she's going to have to listen if she truly cares about you."

Hudson hadn't wanted to listen, but he was willing to listen now. And they were facing the same problem, one that had sunk them in their youth—Stephen's own fears and his obligations to his parents.

Funny, each time he spoke to Melinda, a solution gathered in Stephen's brain, probably because they sat in the same boat, but he was at an age where he could do something about it, whereas Melinda was still under her parents' supervision.

And he knew what he had to do.

CHAPTER TWENTY: JUST A LITTLE LOVE

In ten minutes, Stephen would go live. With the programming already done in advance, he'd have to make one quick change to his show. Hopefully it wouldn't screw up what he'd worked hard to arrange.

His mind was made up. Not only would he play *that* special song for Hudson, but he'd swing by his place after the show. It'd be a late arrival, well after ten, but considering the roller-coaster ride of their tattered relationship, he'd been playing catch-up from day one.

Giving advice and taking his own advice was the reason for their relationship tanking. If Stephen couldn't find the balls to right his many wrongs, he couldn't expect a teenager to dig deep for courage and express her feelings or go after what she wanted.

He'd added *I'll Love You More Than You'll Ever Know*, a special song covered live by Black Oak Arkansas in nineteen seventy-six. It was a great blues number about a man who'd give up everything and change everything about himself for the one he loved. If that didn't give Hudson the hint, Stephen didn't know what would.

Give up everything . . .

Stephen squeezed his eyes shut. This weekend, he'd have to have a long talk with Mom. Hopefully, she'd understand. Yes, he'd come home to help her, but he had a life to see to. She did tell him to go to Hudson. She was trying to manage her disease now.

The beep came. The song Stephen had added was up next.

Straightening in his chair, he leaned forward and set his hands on the desk just as the tune ended.

"That was *Glitter Queen* by Hydra. Next up on tonight's show of obscure southern rock songs is a cover of Blood, Sweat, and Tears' *I Love You More Than You'll Ever Know* by one of my favorite bands, Black Oak Arkansas."

"That's right." He leaned in closer to the mic and softly said, "I love you more than you'll ever know. Stay tuned for *The Friend Song* coming up after this." If those two runs didn't tell Hudson how Stephen felt, he was going to have to get on his knees and beg.

The phone rang. A prickle of annoyance gathered on his skin because he wouldn't get to sink into the chair and lose himself in Jim Dandy's gritty voice belting out how Stephen felt at that moment. He picked up. "You've reached Music from the North, care to share your request?" he asked in his most flirty and friendly voice.

"Yes."

Stephen almost dropped the phone. It was Hudson calling.

"I'd like to hear *Pilot of the Airwaves* by Charlie Dore, and I'd like to dedicate it to my pilot of the airwaves."

Stephen again had to juggle the phone. They both loved the old-school song from nineteen seventy-nine about a girl who spent the night listening to the radio, bonding with the deejay who kept spinning her most beloved music.

"I enjoy phoning in because you always sound different over the airwaves than in person. The pilot I know lets everyone see the real him when he's playing music for us late-nighters, instead of hiding behind a mask his parents forced him to wear. It's the one place where they can't touch you — the airwaves. Maybe that's why they guilted you into becoming a teacher, hey?"

The words spoken couldn't be denied. Stephen bowed his head.

"Funny thing is, I talked to your mother today. She apologized, even admitted she was wrong."

This time Stephen's mouth fell open. "Uh . . . what?"

"I'm serious. We had a long talk before we got into her appointment. Anyway, make sure and play my request, pilot."

The line went dead.

Shaking and baffled, Stephen cued the music into the program to accommodate Hudson's request. It took about five minutes to reset the programming. By then he'd opened a can of iced tea.

Everything happening today was surreal. He tilted the can and sipped. First Mom and now Hudson. What had they specifically talked about? If Mom had gone to bat for him, he'd shit twice and die from embarrassment. No thirty-two-year-old man sent their mother to help them with their failing love life.

A blast of cold air blew into the small room. Stephen swiveled in the chair to see Hudson entering, bundled in enough winter apparel to match the thick fur and hide of a polar bear.

"Are you playing my song?" Hudson slapped his mitts together.

"I just programed it into the lineup." It was a good thing Stephen was drinking iced tea, because the moisture in his mouth and throat vanished.

"I got one more request." Hudson removed his mittens. He then tackled his many layers of clothing.

The way he slid out of his apparel was an enticing invitation to get busy. Too bad Stephen was on the job. He couldn't help licking his lips at Hudson stripped down to his t-shirt and jeans. Even his boots were off to the side. In his socked feet, he strutted forward.

Goosepimples popped up under Stephen's skin.

Hudson closed the distance in the small space and knelt between Stephen's splayed thighs. "So, you love me more than I'll ever know, huh?"

Stephen stiffly nodded as he continued to gape.

"Hurting me, it means you hurt yourself even more?" Hudson walked his fingers up Stephen's thigh while continuing to stare up at him, his question paraphrasing the song.

All Stephen could do was nod again because his voice box had vanished.

"So you wanna be someone I can trust?" Hudson's fingers kept inching closer to Stephen's crotch.

"Uh . . . yeah," Stephen managed to choke out.

"And you wanna be a part of me? A part of me that I only reveal to you?" Hudson's palm rested on Stephen's crotch.

Stephen gritted his teeth. A hot bed of excitement danced inside his jeans. His cock was alive, the tip demanding a caress, a sucking, a kiss. "Yes."

"And you'll be anything I want?" Hudson leaned in and pecked the button to Stephen's pants.

The kiss almost burned straight through the denim. "Anything," Stephen gasped out.

"And you want no one else but me?" Hudson's palm moved over Stephen's groin.

Stephen groaned. His head fell back against the top of the swiveling leather chair, and he nodded.

"Then I'd say you played the right song for me, 'cause I want you in my life. I want you to live up to every word that Jim Dandy sang." Hudson unfastened the button and lowered the zipper to the jeans.

Stephen's cock almost climbed out of his pants. "I'm on the air."

"I don't care. You'll figure it out." Hudson eased Stephen's dick from his underwear.

The song was ending. Before anything more could happen to his cock, Stephen hit the mic and quickly said, "Next up for obscure southern rock songs is *Dancin' Man* by Blackfoot," in a voice dryer and hoarser than the desert.

He laid his head back on the chair just as Hudson's warm lips brushed the tip of his erection.

"You do that well. Very well." Hudson licked Stephen from the base of his dick all the way to the head.

It was only natural Stephen should think of himself as dessert, because not only was the temperature a good minus thirty below, Hudson was loving his prick like a sweaty, hot man baking under the July sun, lapping up a dish of French vanilla ice cream. Even the delectable slurps as Hudson kept licking and sucking was a famished man ready to swallow his meal whole.

"Hmm ... there's lots more that I do well." Hudson brushed his lips back and forth along the head. "Wait'll you find out later."

"Later?" Stephen stole a quick peek at the minutes left on the song.

"My place." Hudson refastened his lips around Stephen's cock.

He was drawn deep into Hudson's mouth, a hot place of slick saliva and wet flesh. Stephen's cock was almost screaming from the pleasure of being in such a luxurious spot feeding him nothing but ecstasy. He pumped his hips, thrusting between Hudson's lips that were locked tight around him. The sucks bestowed on him not only hit him square in the cock but rode up his spine and spread through his limbs.

He couldn't help himself and slid his palms on Hudson's cheeks to get a nice firm hold to fuck his face. Hudson kept his eyes open, and the sparkle in his dark gems said he loved what Stephen was doing.

Stephen couldn't help but move his palms in a circular motion along Hudson's full cheeks since he looked damned handsome with a mouth full of cock and his lips close to grinning.

When Hudson tugged at Stephen's jeans, he managed to wiggle his way partially out of the constricting material to allow full access to his crotch. His groin almost sighed in relief from being fully free. With a sly grin, Hudson lowered the jeans all the way to Stephen's ankles.

"You got the nicest fucking balls." Hudson patted Stephen's sac.

"One . . . one sec." Stephen glanced at the mic. Screw it. He'd let the playlist keep running without introducing any songs. "Never mind. Keep going."

"Yeah? Stroke it?" Hudson ran his finger upward and drew a circle around the most sensitive area of the tip.

The precum being spread around the head of Stephen's cock was torturous teasing. If that wasn't enough, Hudson leaned in and sucked Stephen's dick back into his mouth. His erection sliding between Hudson's lips, wrapped in a slick bath of silk, shot tingles through Stephen's limbs. He jerked and groaned.

The pleasure growing in his crotch was a hot fire ready to explode. Never in his wildest dreams had he believed he'd get a blow job while on the air. His hips bucked on their own, demanding to taste more of the sensual bliss Hudson's mouth offered.

Just as Mama's Pride began playing *Blue Mist,* a burst of ecstatic pleasure ripped through Stephen. He stiffened as he was taken far from the radio station and straight to nirvana where Hudson always took him. He didn't even have time to revel in the aftershock, because Hudson had begun flicking his tongue on the tip of Stephen's dick. The tiny ripples of pleasure kept consuming him, and he cried out while holding tight to Hudson's cheeks.

God, he couldn't get over how Hudson had come over and pleasured him. Stephen's breathing remained rapid, but the declaration easily slid off his tongue, "I love you. I love you more than you'll ever know."

To finally be able to say those words brought more pleasure to Stephen than the blow job.

Dick still in his mouth, Hudson grinned. He released his lips. "I love you, too. I never stopped loving you."

Stephen stroked Hudson's cheek. "Me neither."

Hudson laid his head in Stephen's lap. "I never wanted us to break up." His voice was a delicate crackle. "I wish I woulda been more understanding to what was happening at home for you."

"It's okay." Stephen stroked Hudson's hair. "I should have found my balls to speak up, but I never did." Melinda rolled through his thoughts. "I'm watching a young girl go through the same thing. My fingers are crossed she'll find the courage I didn't have."

"You have courage. Lots of courage. Your problem is you always want to keep the peace with everyone. Even your dad," Hudson murmured. "When your mom stopped by . . ."

"We had a talk this morning over breakfast." Stephen kept stroking Hudson's cheek.

"You know you gotta let her try." Hudson's breath brushed Stephen's dick.

"She's ready to try." Stephen glanced down at Hudson. "I guess the disastrous dinner was for the best."

"It was." Hudson straightened. "If it wasn't for that dinner, we'd still be . . ." He glanced away. "I don't want to think what would've happened. What matters is we're together."

"Yeah, together." Stephen traced the outline of Hudson's mouth that was still wet with spit and maybe some jizz. "I'm going home with you tonight."

"Does this mean I'm sitting in for your show?"

"Of course." Stephen chuckled. "Maybe you can announce a few songs."

"All for it. I always wondered what it'd be like to be on the air." Hudson leaned back and grabbed his jacket. He produced a hankie.

"You're kidding." Stephen laughed. "What did you do — bring lube, too?"

"Nah. Just something to clean you up." Hudson used the handkerchief to rub down Stephen's cock. "We can pillow talk back at my place. There's something else we gotta speak about."

Chapter Twenty-One: Changed by Love

Hudson's head rested on Stephen's warm chest. After two weeks of not getting any, he'd sure had his fill tonight. His lonely house wasn't empty again. Even better, the scent of Stephen's cologne added a wonderful refreshing aroma to the bedroom.

"I'm thinking about adopting a dog and a cat." His lips brushed Stephen's nipple while speaking.

"The rez has enough of them to pick from." Stephen's arm draped Hudson, and he ran his finger along his shoulder.

"We should join that committee. The one for stray rescues. They need a lot of help." If Hudson got any cozier, he'd turn into the plump pillows they were nestled on.

"Good idea. But between work, my radio show, the two-spirit group, and Mom, I'm not sure when I'll have the time."

"Your mother wants to live independently again," Hudson reminded him.

"True." Stephen pecked the top of Hudson's head. "I'm guessing she's finally going to take up the rez on their offer of a personal support worker."

"Is she?"

"I'm assuming she will. She seemed pretty determined this morning to try."

"I'm proud of your mother. Y'know, we all need time to grieve, and not just your dad, either. She needed time to grieve the loss of her health. Some move on right away, while others don't. We all have different grieving periods." If only Hudson could've been more understanding before speaking to Mrs. Brandt this morning. But better late than never.

"You mentioned you had something to talk about." Stephen's voice was mellow.

Yes, Hudson did. He wasn't sure how to broach it while they were cuddling. "Your mom knows how much you love broadcasting. I know how much you love broadcasting. The whole rez knows how much you love broadcasting. The equipment's there. The reserve will support you if you take over Russell's position."

"But they shut down the station. They'd have to start all over again. It's a long process."

"More bureaucratic red tape?" Hudson almost wanted to smack himself upside the head.

"When isn't there red tape? Russel filled me in on everything about remote First Nations operating radio stations. The rez didn't have to apply for a license because they fell under the classification of non-profit. What he did was link up with the radio station based out of Thunder Bay under section B of the Native Broadcasting Policy."

"Is that something we can do again?" Hudson crossed his fingers.

"Of course. The programming wasn't exclusively music, remember? The station was created to address specific native culture and linguistic needs. The Friday night show was our music night. But I operate straight music on my station."

"What if you operated it like Russell did?"

"Then we wouldn't have to apply for a license, but we'd have to stay within the policy, and file a *Promise of Performance*. Oh, it's tons of stuff to weed through, but it's doable."

If it was doable, that meant they'd have the backing to pursue the radio station with a true signal instead of through the Internet. "Then do it. Get it started. I'll help you. Just think, it'll be going twenty-four seven, instead of six to ten."

Stephen chuckled. "I got done telling you how busy I am. When am I supposed to find time to restart the radio station? You know how much work went into that for Russel?"

"But if you were freed up to get the station up and running again . . ." Hudson couldn't resist sucking Stephen's nipple between his teeth.

Stephen let out a half snort and half chuckle. "Hey, that tickles." He teasingly smacked Hudson's shoulder.

Hudson relented. He needed to hear Stephen's answer. "Well?"

"I'm not freed up—"

"If you were freed up."

Stephen let out a breath that blew against the top of Hudson's head. "If I was freed up, yes, I'd get the radio station up and running again."

"That's what you wanted to do all along, right? You wanted to take over Russel's job eventually."

Silence permeated the room.

"Well?" Hudson wormed his way out from Stephen's arm. He propped himself on his elbow to face him. "We're a couple now. We're supposed to share our thoughts and feelings, even our dreams."

"Fine. You got me." Stephen ran his finger along Hudson's cheek. "I want to get the station going again. I always wanted to run the station. I also wanted to deejay."

"And teaching?"

Stephen's mouth sank downward. "That was for my . . . dad." Sincerity then reflected in his gaze. "Don't get me wrong. I enjoy what I do."

"But your dream's deejaying. Managing a radio station."

"Yes." The sincerity in Stephen's gaze changed to regret. "How can I leave my job? The students count on me. The education committee counts on me. You know how hard it is to get teachers up here."

"And that same thought woulda been in your mind if you'd have pursued radio broadcasting instead of your B. Ed?"

A hint of red brightened Stephen's cheekbones. "You're right."

"You can't take on every responsibility on the rez. You also gotta do what's right for you. That's what you spent your life doing—pleasing your parents, pleasing the rez, even trying to please me." Hudson stared at his hand resting on the mattress. "And I was wrong for being as demanding as your parents." He swallowed. "I put as much pressure on you as they did."

"You can't take all the blame. If I had a real backbone, I woulda pushed back against everyone." Stephen kept tracing Hudson's cheek, staring intently. "A person can't be forced unless they have a gun to their head. The fact is, I let my parents push me in a direction I didn't want to go."

"Not true. You love them. Shit, I wish I had parents, maybe then I'd understand better how much you wanna please people who love you." But Hudson did have Stephen's love in his palm, after years of wishing and dreaming. He could finally understand why pleasing others was important. Before, he'd had Kokum, and that was that.

"It's in the past. As you said—we got to move forward now."

"Then let's move forward. Get that radio station going." Hudson couldn't help his pleading.

Stephen pressed his lips together. "It's something I'll think good and hard on once the school year is done. That's a promise."

"You mean the summer?"

Stephen nodded. "The summer. I'll speak to chief and council, ask them about restarting the radio station, and we'll see what happens afterward . . . If it's meant to be, it's meant to be. If it's not . . ."

"That's all I'm asking. Give it a chance. Nothing more." Hudson leaned in and covered Stephen's mouth with his. "It's been two weeks since I last got laid. I need one more round before we sleep."

"Mmm . . . you got it." Stephen drew Hudson onto his chest.

For Sunday dinner, this time the mood in the house wasn't somber. Instead of sitting in her recliner, frowning, Mom was in the kitchen assisting Stephen with preparing the meal before Hudson arrived.

"So what are you going to tell her?" Mom couldn't take three plates from the cupboard since it caused her too much pain and her joints weren't strong enough, but she smiled as she removed them one by one and set them at their place settings on the table.

"As a teacher, I can't interfere. Melinda has to find her own answers, and being a minor, she does have to take her parents into consideration. They are her legal guardians. But if she follows her heart, I know she'll be okay." Stephen already had his little speech he'd give to Melinda after the two-spirit meeting on Monday. No, he couldn't keep her from making painful decisions or save her from hurt, but he could guide her to what lay in her heart. The rest was up to Melinda.

From the corner of his eye, while stirring the gravy on the element, Stephen caught Hudson's truck driving by in the picture window. His heart skipped a beat. He couldn't believe the happiness he'd enjoyed over the last week after getting the greatest *hello* at the radio station.

"Someone's here." Mom's smile was warmer than the gravy simmering on the stove.

Again, Stephen's heartbeat quickened. He couldn't believe the two people he loved most were finally getting along. "So you were saying you were going to accept the CHR's recommendation for a personal support worker?"

He'd been after Mom to say yes to the community health representative's suggestion from the moment his plane had touched down two years ago.

"Yes, it's about time." Mom opened the drawer where the silverware was stored. She withdrew the knives. "You have a life to live . . ."

"Mom . . ."

"No arguing." Mom's voice firmed. She gazed at him. "I was married, I had a husband, raised a son, and had a good life. It's your turn now."

Stephen's face flamed at the *marriage* word. "You're not even sixty."

"But my life's changed. Your dad's gone. I have a chronic disease. I have to figure out how I want to enjoy the last half of my life." She began setting the knives at the place settings. "I can't do that if I have you taking care of me. You need a life of your own."

"I do have a life. I—"

"You know what I mean." Mom reached into the drawer and grabbed the forks just as Hudson knocked at the door.

Stephen left the stove and strode for the utility room. When he opened the back door, his heart almost melted all over the floor at Hudson standing on the other side, again holding a package of bannock. "C'mon in. Supper's almost done. I'm working on the gravy."

"Yeah? Anything else that you're working on for me?" Hudson stepped forward, forcing Stephen to step backward. The bannock was between them that Hudson held.

"Hmm . . . maybe we can discuss it later." Stephen couldn't help leaning in and stealing a brief kiss. Hudson's warm lips easily steamed Stephen's mouth.

"Later? As in *over at my place* later?" Hudson kept his lips on Stephen's.

"Exactly." Stephen took the bannock. "Take off your clothes and make yourself comfy."

"I'll remember those words when we go to my place after supper." Hudson snickered. He unzipped his parka.

Stephen couldn't help chuckling as he ambled back into the kitchen with the bannock.

"Oh, how nice." Mom's dark eyes glowed. "Bannock."

"Specially made for you," Hudson said while he entered the kitchen in his socked feet. His hair was tied back.

"Specially made for you is black tea." Mom shuffled to the counter. "I have it steeping. I thought you might want something to drink before we eat."

"All for it." Hudson turned over the teacup at his place setting as he sat at the table.

"You sit, too," Mom ordered.

Stephen shrugged and pulled out the chair at his spot.

Mom hefted the teapot off the counter. Because her hands shook, the porcelain vessel vibrated like an earthquake had come to the reserve. Even the lid rattled.

"You have to also know when to ask for help." Stephen scrambled from his chair.

Mom sighed. Her hands loosened on the teapot Stephen eased from her clutches. "Now that I want to try, it gets frustrating when I . . . oh well. I guess I'll have to adjust."

"It's okay." Stephen filled their cups. "You're doing the best you can."

"I simply wanted to make a toast." Mom sat in her chair.

"A toast?" Hudson squinted.

"Yes. A toast." Mom fixed her tea.

"A toast to what?" Once he filled everyone's cups, Stephen sat.

"A toast to you and you." Mom's gaze moved from Hudson and then to Stephen.

"To us?" Stephen set his hand on his chest.

"Yes." Mom flushed. She pinned her warm stare on Hudson. "It may sound corny, but I want to thank you."

"Thank me?" Hudson's brows knitted even further.

"For making my son happy. I've never seen him happier. He's been skipping around this house all week, his feet barely touching the floor." Mom smiled.

Stephen almost coughed. He gaped at his mother. "Oh geez, you don't need to give him all the details."

"Yes, I do. I want him to know he makes you happy, and if you're happy, then I'm happy. So thank you for giving this place a much-needed boost of good energy. For so long it's been . . . well, it hasn't been the happiest place after Brad . . . passed. We needed this change. We really did."

"You don't have to thank me, Mrs. Brandt." Hudson raised his teacup. "I should thank you. You said your house had some dreary energy, what do you think mine was? It sure wasn't a bottle of sunshine after Kokum died. Now?" He winked at Stephen. "The sun's shining there all the time."

"How about to all three of us. I'd say we finally found our way. Haven't we?" Yes, Stephen could agree on that. As a trio, they'd been unhappy and lost. And now they had finally found their path, and the strange thing was, the path had led them back to where they belonged.

Epilogue: Back on the Track

On his snowmobile, Hudson plowed through the fresh February snow, maneuvering the growling machine up the one bank and then hurling it up and over the slope to finally come to a rest in the small parking lot at the radio station. He pulled up beside his husband's SUV.

He still had to pinch himself. A married man, a newlywed, having done the deed on New Year's Eve. Never did he imagine last winter he'd have this shiny, brand-new, beautiful life.

He removed his helmet and sidled into the radio station to Stephen at the mic and *Ma'iingan* thumping his tail, tongue hanging out. Hudson's heart warmed at the newest addition to his growing family, having aptly named the stray dog because he did resemble a wolf with his gray-and-white coloring, triangle-shaped ears, double-layered coat, and big paws.

Stephen switched off the mic and turned. He had the tip of a pen in his mouth, legs slightly parted, and elbow resting on the arm of the chair. "Well, hello, hello. Did you bring us dinner?"

"I'm on the sled. It'd get super-cold, but I do have a pot of stew simmering." Hudson strolled over, petting *Ma'iingan*'s thick head of fur while planting a kiss on Stephen's mouth. "And I baked you some fresh bannock."

"Sounds delish." Stephen grinned. "I'll be home in an hour. Did you wanna take him for a run? I think he's getting bored hanging out with me."

"That's why I'm here." Hudson glanced at the dog who

thumped its tail. "I came right over once I got supper going."

"How'd work go?" Stephen asked.

"Great. And how are you enjoying your work?" Hudson couldn't believe Stephen was the manager of the reserve's brand-new radio station, kicked off at the beginning of the new year.

"You know me. I can't get enough of being on the air. I just wish I had more time on the mic. But I enjoyed every minute training the other two deejays."

Stephen held up his finger. "One second." He flipped on the mic. "Stay tuned for the next hour for more music. Coming up at six, Greg will be here with lessons on your culture. Tonight, he's discussing the history of the jingle dress and its importance to the People. Now here is an oldie and obscure from Lynyrd Skynyrd. *Swamp Music*. That's right. Instead of listening to *Sweet Home Alabama*, flip the record over and dive into track six on their *Second Helping* album."

The funky tune began playing.

Stephen joined his fingers together, palms facing Hudson, stretched out his hands, and cracked his knuckles.

"Tired? I was listening to you all afternoon at the nursing station."

"Somewhat. But not tired enough to . . . sleep." Stephen chuckled.

"If you don't want to crash in front of the couch and watch TV, I take it it'll only be the three of us instead of four." Hudson couldn't help waggling his brows.

"Yeah. Mom's going to bingo with Fred."

"Fred? Again?" Hudson snickered. "Those two seem to be getting pretty cozy."

Stephen shrugged. "I'm keeping my nose out of it. Mom says they're good friends. If anything happens, it happens. I'm simply glad she's got quite the social life going again."

"Then I'll see you at home." Hudson stole another kiss,

brushing his lips against Stephen's warm mouth.

"Okay. Maybe we can have dessert first before dinner?" Teasing was in Stephen's suggestion. "I'll scrub your back if you scrub mine?"

"You got it." Hudson couldn't stop smiling. He picked up his snowmobile helmet and whistled at *Ma'iingan*. "A hot bubble bath is what will be waiting when you get home." Then he said to their dog, "C'mon, boy. Time for your run."

With *Ma'iingan* on his heels, Hudson left the radio station and walked back out into the cold chill. His boots crunched along the shoveled path. The air was crisp, and his breaths left white puffs.

Not a hint of a breeze was present. The sun had set long ago, and the lights from the houses populating Main lit the reserve. A truck puttered by, and Hudson raised his arm, waving.

Yes, there was no better place to be other than . . . home. He truly was back where he belonged. Once Stephen finished work, Hudson would suggest they start planning their honeymoon they'd kept putting off. Maybe next year at this time they could head south, enjoy some time in Mexico or the Caribbean. Or even take a cruise. Anything to get away from another cold winter.

The possibilities for where to celebrate their wedding were endless. More than celebrate their wedding. Celebrate spending the rest of their lives together.

You May Also Enjoy the Following from eXtasy Books Inc:

TWO PRINCES
Maggie Blackbird
June 12, 2022

To win over the chief's haughty son, a drug-dealing punk from a dysfunctional family must risk the only two things he has: his reputation and freedom.

Blurb

Billy Redsky, a rebellious punk who loves art and nature, is saddled with a welfare-leeching, alcoholic mother and criminal older brother who are the joke of their Ojibway community. Sick and tired of being perceived as a loser, Billy deals drugs for his older brother to earn quick money. He hopes if he buys a dirt bike, he'll finally impress the chief's popular and aloof son, René Oshawee.

When the two are forced to serve detention together, a friendship begins to bloom, but much to Billy's frustration, René keeps putting him on ice. To make his biggest dream come true if he finally wants to call René his own, Billy must make a huge decision that could cost him everything.

Billy leaned in. "Why you're being a jerk to me? I came over here to see you. We have biz to finish."

"What biz?"

"What happened on the lunch hour."

"You got high. Duh. Or were you too stoned to remember?" Sarcasm and icicles clung to René's cold words.

"Never mind that. When we were staring at each other." Billy tapped on the counter.

"Staring?" René snorted. "Get off it. I got work to do. Maybe if you'd slow down on the toking, your brain might function properly." He turned the key on the till and hit a few buttons on the keyboard. The printer shoved out paper, and the cash draw banged open. "Don't steal anything while I'm locking the door."

"Fuck you." Billy spun on his heel as René strode to the entrance.

"Well, you got a rep as a thief." René locked the deadbolt and returned to the counter, nostrils still flaring slightly.

This time Billy banged on the counter. "Something's up your ass, and I'm not leaving until you tell me."

"There's nothing to tell." René dumped the change on the counter. He started counting the quarters.

"There is, too. Like how you were looking at me." Billy leaned in farther and caught a whiff of the crisp cologne.

René stopped counting. He slowly raised his head. His eyebrows straightened into a flat line of disgust. "You must've dropped acid on the lunch hour, 'cause now you're hallucinating."

"Hallucinating?" Billy pointed at his chest. "Nope. Not hallucinating. There're times when you look at me. *Really* look at me. You did it when we had our dust-up in the hallway and got sent to detention. You did it again when we stopped at the light before we went up the mountain. You did it when Cinnamon Bear decided to eat our munchies. And you did it yesterday when you were flipping out 'cause I got high . . ."

René's jawline twitched, and he curled his fingers into a fist.

" . . . and I totally dig when you look at me *that* way," Billy finished, heart beating fast enough to almost burst through his ribs. Sweat slithered down his back. "I wish you'd keep looking at me *that* way." The last of his words came out soft.

There. He'd found his balls to say his piece, and his damned mouth had gone dry.

By the twitch of René's upper lip, Billy had bombed big-time. He was probably going to get a punch in the face to match the fading bruises on his cheeks.

René drummed his fingers on the counter.

Billy held his breath. Never was he so aware of the passing of time. One second. Two seconds. Three seconds. The air had gone still. He couldn't swallow. He couldn't move. He kept staring at René, who was focused beyond Billy's shoulder. There was hope.

"I . . ." René's pink tongue slithered along his lower lip, glistening, seeming to dare Billy to taste.

ABOUT THE AUTHOR

An Ojibway from Northwestern Ontario, Maggie resides in the country with her husband and their fur babies, two beautiful Alaskan Malamutes. When she's not writing, she can be found pulling weeds in the flower beds, mowing the huge lawn, walking the Mals deep in the bush, teeing up a ball at the golf course, fishing in the boat for walleye, or sitting on the deck at her sister's house, making more wonderful memories with the people she loves most.

Web Site: https://maggieblackbird.com/
Facebook Page: https://www.facebook.com/maggieblackbirdauthor/
Twitter: https://twitter.com/BlackbirdMaggie/
Goodreads: https://www.goodreads.com/maggieblackbird
BookbBub: https://www.bookbub.com/profile/maggieblackbird
Linked In: https://www.linkedin.com/in/maggie-blackbird-032798169/
Instagram: https://www.instagram.com/maggieblackbirdauthor/
eXtasy Books Author Page: https://www.extasybooks.com/maggie-blackbird/
Newsletter Sign-Up: eepurl.com/gJu2VL

www.ingramcontent.com/pod-product-compliance
Lightning Source LLC
Chambersburg PA
CBHW060816120626
46557CB00001B/239